PRAISE FOR MERIDEL NEWTON

"A gripping, tense standoff in a dystopian future where survival of the fittest might just take a whole community." —Suzanne Palmer

"Newton has developed a robust world that creates high stakes for her social experiment and sets the stage for a shift in mindset." —Rowan Hill, reviewer

"Though the message is about how cooperation will be the salvation of the human race, *The Shelter Trilogy* doesn't paint a rosy, fluffy picture. It is refreshing to read a realistic, hopeful take on the post-apocalyptic trend." —Gabrielle Contelmo, reviewer

I0733828

THE PRESENT DAY BY DAY

THE SHELTER TRILOGY II

MERIDEL NEWTON

THE FUTURE SECOND BY SECOND

Edited by Holly Lyn Walrath.

Cover design by Holly Lyn Walrath.

Published by Interstellar Flight Press, Houston, Texas.

www.interstellarflightpress.com

ISBN (eBook): 978-1-953736-51-2

ISBN (Paperback): 978-1-953736-50-5

First Edition: 2026

CONTENTS

DAY 1

Amaya Bly needed her routines. She trusted them. Relied on them, even. She needed her mornings to be slow and filled with family—leading the children through their Fajr prayers while Cedric brought them all mugs of whatever tea the kitchens were brewing, listening to the life of the Shelter waking up around them, going through her lists and memos to preview the day to come. She needed the calm, the familiar, the simple, to fortify her for the chaos of the coming day.

She had led the village of Osto through a long and difficult winter to this first flourishing promise of spring. Despite her initial misgivings, four months ago she had taken the reins from Vasha when the old Headwoman ardently declared her wish to retire. Vasha named Amaya her preferred successor, and the vote had been almost pro forma—only Stan Johnson had run against her, and he spent the entire time loudly proclaiming that he had no actual desire to lead but believed that no election should ever be one sided. She had won easily, praise be.

Even the remnants of Esteben's Men had acquiesced, much to the surprise of the original villagers. The former raiders spent the winter proving their use to the village: slowly integrating themselves into the daily scheduling of chores, repairing some of the crumbling outlying buildings to make stables for their horses and a new smithy for George, and sharing what weapons and supplies they'd brought with their newly adopted home.

She'd known that accepting the position of Headwoman meant surrendering her days and evenings to the village. Her nights and mornings, though—those belonged to her and her family. And if her mornings lingered a little longer than was strictly necessary, if she dragged her feet down the halls to the front of the Shelter, well, who could blame her? Some days, she simply needed a little more time to prepare for all those who would demand she bleed for them.

Which was why she found she had less patience than she usually would when she was confronted in the hallway between her allotment and the communal kitchens.

"We need to talk about Anton."

Elise Johnson was a sturdy woman, practical and realistic. In a village of obligate farmers, she and her husband, Stan, stood out as people who would have chosen to work the land in any world—up to and including one better than this. She was dour and practical, focused on the numbers and logistics of production. How she had managed to raise the most dreamy, romantic child in the Shelter was something Amaya would never understand.

"Of course, Elise. How did Anton handle his rotation on patrol?"

"He *didn't*." The woman glowered. "Stan took him right up to the barn every day but couldn't get him to go in. Devra ended up assigning him to clean tack all week. And I know Sarah says his hand is all healed, but you can't tell me that's good for it! What were you *thinking* with that assignment?"

Amaya tried to cover her wince. "I was thinking that it would be good to give him something active to do. Devra's a good patrol leader. She would have looked after him out there."

"Out there! On patrol with a bunch of raiders—"

"Newcomers."

"—Newcomers, that the boy can barely look at! Really, Amaya. Don't you understand his condition?"

She sighed. The truth was, she *did* understand Anton Johnson. The boy had been the most gifted weaver Osto had ever seen, and had enjoyed a number of privileges as a result— such as avoiding patrol duty in favor of extra rotations on the looms. But last summer, one of the new arrivals had disabled his favored hand in an incident still contested by those who had witnessed it. And though his hand was supposedly well healed, his confidence had yet to recover anywhere near as well.

"If he just gave it a chance, he might like patrol," she tried. "It's active, involved, it gets him out of the Shelter, it teaches survival skills—"

"He's had those skills since he was a child!" Elise interrupted. "Anton's done every job in Osto, same as any child here, and he found what he was good at. You can't condemn him to a life of misery just because of one bad hand!"

"No one wants that, Elise," Amaya said. Her patience was wearing thin. She shifted from one foot to the other. "But we can't find him a new place if he won't *try*—"

"He is trying! More than you know! He's—"

Earthquakes don't always start as shaking or swaying. Sometimes, they start as a ripple of water in a cup or the skittering of a dish on a shelf. This one started with just the slightest shift of the ground beneath her feet—between one step and the next, her weight already committed, Amaya found the solid surface of the earth was not where it should have been, and she pitched forward with a startled cry.

Elise had just enough warning to open her arms to catch her. With a moment to steady herself, Amaya straightened up and caught her breath.

Then the shaking started in earnest.

"What is—?"

"Earthquake!" Elise gasped. "What? Here?"

It was early enough that most of the population of the Shelter was still present, lingering over their breakfast or savoring the last bit of quiet. As the building shook and jumped, the quiet was shattered by the sounds of not only human distress, but the protest of twisting metal and the crash of ceramic. Amaya gave herself a full second of animal panic before her rational mind took over.

This was Osto. This was the Shelter. And they had contingency plans for circumstances like these.

"Elise, go find the south lot captain! Make sure all are accounted for. Go!"

Elise took a quick, deep breath, nodded, and dashed off. Amaya found herself both surprised and grateful for the instant obedience, but she didn't let it slow her down as she pivoted on one foot and sprinted for the back of the building. As she ran, she yelled.

"Captains! Count your people! Everyone out! No one left behind!"

She hit the back hallway as the building alarm finally kicked in. Even as she took a moment to catch her breath, other voices rose throughout the building.

"North lots at the captain's room!"

"South lots at the kitchens!"

"East lots at the east wall!"

"West lots at the west wall!"

A door opened slowly down the hallway, and Amaya caught her breath in relief as Vasha emerged from her room, whole and hale.

"I suppose everything was going too smoothly, eh?" she quipped, and Amaya almost managed a laugh.

"Out through the back, then, Vasha?" she asked, offering her arm to the older woman.

The former Headwoman pulled a face at this, but nodded. Cane on one side and Amaya on the other, they made good time through the Shelter's barn.

"No one's assigned to release the animals, are they?" Vasha asked as they trotted past the pens of nervous sheep and goats.

"We'll add that to the drills for next time," Amaya answered, her jaw set and her gaze fixed on the back door.

"Better not," Vasha said. "No point in upsetting them any more than necessary."

Amaya nodded. There was no point in pretending there wouldn't be a next time. Better to assume that anything that could go wrong, would. That was the only reason Osto had survived as long as it had.

By the time they reached the front, the lot captains were already lining up their people in the plaza and checking over their lists with the duty roster to determine whether absences were due to early patrol rounds or less fortunate circumstances.

Amaya felt a surge of pride in her people and their training. It had been maybe three minutes since the first jolt of the quake—maybe four, she amended, glancing at Vasha. Yet there they all were, lined up and waiting, silent and tense, but all seemingly present and uninjured, Oston and newcomer alike.

Both Vasha and Amaya made for the knot of captains without having to exchange a word, even as the stones continued to shift and roll beneath their feet. The reports were almost calming—all was as well as could be expected under the circumstances. Everyone was out and safe, and the only people missing were those known to be on patrol.

Almost calm. Amaya allowed herself a moment to breathe, relief washing over her.

That was when the shouting arose from the direction of the outlying buildings. "Fire! Fire! Help!"

All whirred into motion, and the village of Osto leaped to action once again.

———

One last, drowsy bee floated gently to the ground, its ever-present buzz stuttering to a stop. Danica watched its entire descent before double-checking her thick gloves, taking a deep breath of herby smoke, and reaching for the small knob low on the beehive. Nothing challenged her, and she grasped and pulled with more confidence than she truly felt. The drawer slid out, smooth as anything, exposing its sticky treasure to the sunlit morning.

She grinned in satisfaction. Narrow but long, the entire interior of the drawer had been carefully cleaned, then covered and subdivided into thousands of tiny eight-sided chambers, all waiting to be filled with golden yellow sweetness. Some cells held a few drops of new nectar, settling in for its long cure; the bees already seeking out the first spring flowers to harvest. As she watched, new honey dripped down the sides of the drawer to pool at the bottom.

An incalculable luxury.

Casting a quick glance over her shoulder, she slipped a padded glove off one hand, dipped a finger in the precious bounty, and brought it to her lips.

Sweetness coated her tongue and tingled down her throat, a warm glow answering from her belly. A yell crept its way up her spine until she couldn't resist letting it out, an overloud whoop of delight that rang against the clouded sky. Her cry startled a crow from its perch overhead, and it launched itself with a raucous call. Danica gave a rueful wince at that, but could not suppress her delight as she sucked the last of the sweet from her finger.

Guilty pleasure accomplished, she carefully replaced the drawer. The colony had already made a good start on the early spring wildflowers, but the honey was nowhere near ready to harvest. The back of the beehome fully opened, revealing a full society of sleeping, satiated bees. She checked over the combs inside, noting honey cells, drone cells, and open holes in the comb—not too many, not enough to worry her. There, in the corner, was the mass of bodies that protected the queen.

And there—she peered closer and almost gave another surprised, pleased cry.

Instead, she carefully closed the beehome, double-checking the latch before she left it. Just as she readied herself to leave, she paused a moment. Then she opened the drawer again, selected the corner with the greatest number of filled cells, and broke off a tiny piece, five or ten in total.

"Thank you," Danica whispered at the colony, half-amused. "We all have our mouths to feed." She collected the smoking bundle of herbs from the ground near the hive and cheerfully made her way up the path to the small cottage she called home.

Her wife, Lani, greeted her at the wattle gate, holding a plump baby in a simple linen one-piece.

"Hey, Mama," Lani said, and the baby gurgled.

"Yes, Chloe, bees!" Danica answered, waving the still-smoking herbs.

The girl gave her a wide-eyed smile.

"We're going to spoil you so much, child," Danica muttered, smiling back. She paused as if in thought, turned around, and made a quick adjustment. When she turned back, she offered two closed fists to her daughter.

"Which one?"

Chloe eyed both fists with wide-eyed solemnity.

"Which one, Chloe?" Danica jiggled her left hand just a little.

"Aah!" The child did not seem to know what else was required of her.

Lani giggled. "What do we say, Chloe?"

The girl paused, her dark eyes confused. "Bah?"

Danica laughed despite herself. "And?"

The wide eyes stared back. "Ahh!"

"There we go." She opened her fist, revealing the bit of honeycomb, sticky and oozing. She held it to Chloe's mouth, and the child closed her lips around it, sucking greedily.

"Can you just imagine growing up never knowing that sugar was a rare thing?" Lani's soft drawl broke into Danica's contemplation of their daughter, perfectly verbalizing her own nascent thoughts.

After a tumultuous winter, Lani had truly found her place in the life of Osto. She had pursued every skill and craft the village had to teach her, and continued to experiment semi-successfully with a few ideas of her own—food preservation had become an unexpected passion, along with the discovery (or rediscovery) of new flavors and tastes. She had recovered from the trial of birth and filled out well since, her brown face becoming plump and round, her arms strong, her curly dark hair lush. But over and above the physical thriving, there was a certain glow to her that spoke of happiness and comfort—of safety, of peace. She had a home—*they* had a home. Together. It may only be a small one-room outlying building just out of sight of Osto's cultivated fields, but it was real, and it was all theirs. Danica had built most of it herself, and they both worked to make it the perfect place to raise their young daughter.

"It doesn't have to be." Danica smiled. "I think the hive is making a new queen. We might try dividing it before it swarms."

"So soon?" Lani raised her eyebrows and opened the gate. "Everyone in Osto will have their own hive."

"I'd give one to every family in the world if I could," Danica said. "No child should grow up without knowing sweetness."

"Maybe we could make it a communal hive. Talk to Headwoman Amaya, put it up on the roof with Ahmed's garden—oh!" Lani's suggestion was cut short as Danica strode forward and caught her up in her arms.

Lani shifted their daughter to a hip and melted into the embrace, and for a moment, all was perfect: still, warm, and golden. They had a home, a family, a community—the horrors that had once threatened her life and her daughter were behind them. The child's father was better forgotten—best never acknowledged, really—the sun had never felt warmer than it had the moment they were out from under his shadow. The winter was over, and their future held untold promise.

Then she shuddered—or she didn't. The *ground* shuddered, moving under her feet with a sudden, alarming liquidity. Her grip on Chloe tightened until the child protested.

"What's happening?" Lani cried.

"I think it's an earthquake!"

"Here?!"

Danica stared as the fence, a cobbled-together mess meant only to keep a small child from wandering too far, shuddered and seemed to uproot itself.

"What do we do?"

"I think, get out from under the trees?"

The world shook around them as they moved, hand-in-hand, toward the path. They wanted to run, but the ground beneath them was untrustworthy, there one second and dropping an inch the next, rendering any attempt at speed futile. Instead, they bumbled through the sudden chaos, and their small world was made unfamiliar and hostile. Trees tossed their branches as though in struggle, and the clatter of boards and roof tiles made the small cottage seem to scream.

The ground jumped, and Lani fell forward, nearly dropping Chloe. Danica caught them both, taking two or three steps back before planting her feet firmly.

"Ahhh . . ."

Lani and Danica both looked down at the plaintive voice, a centering force in the chaos.

Big brown eyes peered up at them both.

Lani gave a sharp bark of laughter and cuddled her daughter closer. "I don't know, baby girl. I don't know."

———

Ahmed shifted in the saddle, trying to find a position that didn't feel like he was being split up the middle. He was new to riding, and he wasn't particularly good at it—and he didn't want to do it enough to *become* good at it. But George had insisted they bring the horses, and Amaya had agreed, and Ahmed had known that if he wanted this trip to actually happen, he'd have to go along with it, so he did. He still wasn't sure he really trusted an animal five times his size to actually listen to him (well, okay, four times—he'd grown like a weed over the winter and now, at thirteen, his arms always seemed to end up in places they shouldn't, and his legs couldn't sit straight in any normal chair), but they'd given him the calmest horse they had, and so long as he stayed behind George, it would hopefully just do whatever George's horse did.

Hopefully.

George glanced back over his shoulder. "It helps if you actually put your feet in the stirrups," he called.

"How can that *possibly* help?" Ahmed grumped. "That seems like a good way to twist an ankle."

George laughed at that. "In the unlikely event that nag tried to throw you, you'd have worse things to worry about, I promise."

"It could *throw* me?"

There was a long silence before George answered, "If you balance in the stirrups, you can stand up in them a bit. And if you do that, we can actually try going a bit faster."

"You say that like it's a good thing!" Ahmed clutched the reins tighter and fixed his gaze on the horse's bobbing ears. "This is fast enough."

"This is a walk, kid," George said, but he sounded cheerful enough that Ahmed didn't worry too much.

They had plenty to be cheerful about. It was a gorgeous morning on a gorgeous early spring day, the kind that either preceded one last winter storm or signaled that warm weather had finally arrived. They rode through a forest of thick undergrowth, with light green buds on the trees and new tips adorning bush and vine. There was no path to follow, but the horses were good at choosing the easiest footing, and they didn't seem too bothered by thorn or burr. So long as they stayed on course (Ahmed checked his compass again—northeast, good), they should find their destination sometime this morning.

Their destination—the river. And *that* would be the beginning of everything. Ahmed fell happily into his favorite daydream. The river would be perfect, fast and shallow, with a defined stone bank to build on. They'd find a site to set up their first water wheel, a simple proof of concept that could lead to so much more. Once they had the wheel, they could start a mill, and suddenly, they would be able to produce more flour and bread. They'd be able to feed everyone without worry. Osto would be secure, and no one would grumble about the raiders, and George could stay—

"Kid, hey, stop your horse."

Ahmed snapped out of his daydream a second too late, but luckily, his horse seemed to be paying attention better. It came to a sudden stop behind George's mount without any encouragement.

"Why? Are we here?" Ahmed looked around, but so far as he could tell, there was nothing to differentiate this stretch of forest from any other.

"Maybe. I'm not sure. But there's something . . . Better dismount."

Ahmed watched closely as George matched action to word, swinging one leg fluidly over the beast's neck and sliding to the ground. He was a big man, but he moved with the easy familiarity of long practice.

Ahmed had been shown how to dismount. He'd even done it a few times before, with assistance and a stool to aim for. Now, he attempted to imitate George's motion, swinging a leg over—but somehow he miscalculated, and he ended up facing into the saddle and the horse's flank as he clutched at flaps and straps, one foot awkwardly caught in the stirrup as he hopped desperately on the other.

"Whoa! I got you, don't worry." George caught him under both armpits and held him there while he disentangled his foot, then lowered him slowly to the ground.

Ahmed hunched his shoulders in shame. "I had it."

"You didn't," George answered, "and if you keep that up, you'll break a leg before you figure it out. Don't pretend otherwise. Just take the time to learn properly."

"I . . . I will." Ahmed looked away, hoping the warmth in his face wasn't as obvious as it felt.

"Quiet now. Follow me."

For all his size, George could move silently when he wanted to. Probably a result of his training with the raiding group Esteben's Men in the years before they'd come to Osto. Ahmed wondered, as he often did, just how much of a gulf existed between him and his closest friend. They understood each other on a level he'd never experienced with anyone else, but they came from such different parts of the world and had such different past lives. Ahmed frequently found himself stopping short, surprised by a display of skill or knowledge he'd never had any reason to acquire.

Which was to say that while George moved quickly and quietly through the underbrush, Ahmed seemed to trip over every root and impale himself on every thorn in his path. Though he followed George's exact footsteps, he slowed, carefully pushing aside whip-thin branches and ducking under loops of vines that the bigger man seemed to hardly notice.

He was so focused on the simple act of walking that he didn't realize George had stopped until he was just a foot or two away. George held an arm out, catching Ahmed across the chest, and held his other hand to his lips.

"What is it?" Ahmed whispered.

George crooked his head down at the slope before them and pulled a close-knit bundle of thin branches lower. Ahmed stood on his tiptoes to see through, and his eyes widened.

Ahead of them, the forested land transitioned into grassy plain and low scrub, then sloped into a narrow strip of rock and mud before dipping into the glassy waters of a broad, calm river.

And on that plain, a small village of tents, huts, and large, covered wagons had sprung up, with people of all ages busying themselves amidst the structures.

George pointed to a pole erected at the far edge of the village. "Do you see what I see?"

Ahmed squinted. ". . . Laundry?"

George laughed, a soft rumble. "Flags."

"Flags?" Ahmed gave the camp a second, more discerning look. "Do you recognize them?"

"Not a one, but anyone with cloth and dye can make a flag. Doesn't mean anything." George frowned to himself for a second. "No, it means they have something to fight for. We shouldn't get any closer."

"Ugh." Ahmed crossed his arms, considering the situation. He'd been so excited to advance their plans for the water wheel, to finally be taking real steps to help the village, start to work toward the creation of electricity, and now—now this most mundane of obstacles. He pulled a face. "Maybe we could try further down the river?"

George shook his head. "Wouldn't risk it. We don't know what they're like. If they've claimed a lot of land, we won't be able to build anywhere near here."

"But . . ." Ahmed heard his voice rising and paused to regain control. "What if they're friendly?"

"We don't know yet, kid. They might be. In my experience, people are a lot friendlier when they see you as equals. And they're more likely to do that if we have more people with us."

Ahmed frowned, but not in disagreement. This was George's area of expertise, not his. He just wanted to build things. Inventions were easy. People were . . . harder.

George gave him a rueful smile. "We're lucky they haven't seen us already. Let's go, kid. This trip's gotten as far as it's going."

"We've barely started," Ahmed said bitterly. He turned, leading the way back to the horses.

Riding once again, frustration surged through Ahmed. He hunched over the saddle and throttled the desire to yell, punch something, or curse. The emotion was so strong he could feel his whole body shaking with it.

Or not. That shaking wasn't coming from inside him at all. "George?"

The big man shook his head, wide eyes fixed on the rustling branches above. "Earthquake! Try to find somewhere clear!"

The horses caught their fear and bolted. Ahmed clung tight and squeezed his eyes closed as the tree trunks began to sway and the canopy turned into a roiling, waving mass of green.

———

Despite her initial misgivings on stepping into power four months ago, Amaya had slowly settled into her title as the new Headwoman. The position had its difficulties, to be sure. Even with Vasha's wisdom to guide her, Amaya had not been prepared to run short on root vegetables or candle wax. Balancing personalities and skills in the duty schedule was an unexpected challenge. Vasha seemed to have an intimate knowledge of all the petty squabbles and old grudges in the village, but Amaya despaired of ever learning them all. And, of course, there were always thornier situations yet, inherited complications with no real right answer.

Like the one before her right now.

"The whole place is broken down," Jacob Newsome repeated. "Collapse started with the quake, then the fire spread from a broken lamp. We can fix it, but we need somewhere to stay now."

Jacob seemed to be the appointed mouthpiece for the whole outlier Newsome clan now arrayed in front of her. Jonathan and Sarah Newsome had had five sons and a daughter while they were together, and four of those sons were already married and working on families of their own. Silent children clung to the skirts of tired-looking women. Jonathan himself, a new bruise spreading across his cheek, stood at the forefront, shoulder-to-shoulder with Jacob, but seemingly content to let his eldest do the talking. Sarah and Eric, Amaya noted, had elected not to join their estranged family during this rare appearance at the Shelter.

"We're low on space here," Amaya said, trying to get her head around the problem. It was too soon after salah to face this. "The raiders —the newcomers—have us packed to the ceiling. There's . . . twenty of you?"

"Twenty-four," Jacob said, nodding at a woman holding a baby that couldn't be more than a few months old. "But we don't all need to stay here. Just the youngest, the rest of us can camp until the house is ready. But . . ."

Amaya followed his gaze to Jonathan. The Newsome patriarch had terrorized her and her family for years. It was entirely his doing that the Blys still lived in the Shelter, when they'd made a bid for their own outlying building years ago. That simmering anger was the first thing she felt anytime she thought about the elder Newsome, but now . . . now she was the village's Headwoman.

She couldn't let herself be only angry at the man who had made it his mission to deny her children rooms of their own.

She had to be *fair* to him as well. Luckily, Vasha had taken some steps to make that at least a bit easier.

"He's still got six months in lockup before he's welcome back," she said.

"How's he supposed to be locked up when we don't got a room with a lock?" Jacob frowned, looking bullish. "We were keeping him separate, just like you said, but we can't now."

It was a definite issue. Rooms with doors were in short supply in Osto. The Shelter itself was mostly one giant indoor space, partitioned only a few times: the barn in the back, which housed most of the village's animals at night, the few small rooms along the walls mostly given to storage (and one still claimed by Vasha as prior-Headwoman's privilege), and the village infirmary which had been built against an outer wall, with no internal connection to the main space of the Shelter.

And none of those would do for a makeshift prison. Loathsome as the man was, he deserved better than to live among the animals for months. She wouldn't trust him alone with any of their precious, dwindling food stores. And the infirmary was right out—she would no more force Sarah to deal with her ex-husband than she'd allow him into her own allotment. Keeping Jon in his own home under house arrest had seemed an ideal solution. Let him use the luxury of that big private house he'd fought so hard for, let his family look after him so that he couldn't bother any of the good, hardworking people of Osto—and he couldn't attempt to foment any more trouble in the fragile alliance with the newcomers.

The thought of the newcomers sparked an idea, though. With the help of the former raiders, Ostons had repaired and built more outlying buildings than ever before in its long history. Some of those structures had been claimed for non-residential purposes—stables, craftrooms, and workshops. One of them, surely, must have space to spare for Osto's only criminal.

"Put him in my room for now."

Amaya startled, and turned to see that Vasha herself had joined the group. The former Headwoman had taken the winter hard—her limp, always present, had turned painful, and her layers of robes and coats hung lank on her frame in a way they never had before. But she still moved with purpose, still set her jaw stubbornly, and still possessed a steely glare that no one, not even Amaya herself, dared to cross.

"Oh, no, Vasha, we couldn't!"

"Don't be silly," she tutted, leaning hard on her cane. "It's only temporary, right? Until you can find space in one of the new crafthalls or some such. I can stay with one of the other families."

Amaya's mouth quirked. Of course the old woman had followed her train of thought. It was at least somewhat gratifying that they had come to the same conclusion.

"You lot can take him back there and lock him in. He knows the way, don't you, Jon?" Vasha raised an eyebrow at the jab.

Jonathan lifted his upper lip in an ugly sneer but said nothing.

Jacob put an arm around his father in a manner that could have been supportive or could have been restraining. "All right. Thankee, ma'am. Ma'ams. We'll get everything back in proper order as soon as we can."

Amaya heaved a sigh. Fair. Right. "Osto will, of course, supply you with anything you need to rebuild your home, Jacob. Now that it's warming up, we have plenty of timber, and I can assign a work rotation to help with construction."

Jacob stared, as did several other members of the family. They clearly hadn't been planning on asking for assistance, and definitely hadn't expected it to be offered.

"We'll take nothing from you, woman," Jon spat out.

"Ah. Let's get you put away, Pa," Jacob said, his grip on the older man's shoulders tightening. They wheeled around, but Jon managed to free himself enough to turn and glare back at Amaya and Vasha.

"Nothing!" he repeated. "We don't need anything from this cursed place, and we won't take it. You arrogant—"

"Come *on*, Pa," Jacob insisted. As he drew his father away, the rest of the Newsomes closed ranks behind him, hiding the ranting wretch from sight.

Amaya closed her eyes, seeking to regain some balance. "You didn't have to do that," she said into the resulting darkness.

"It was the fastest way to get rid of him, wasn't it?" Vasha answered.

A hard rap and subsequent footsteps indicated that Vasha was moving away. Amaya opened her eyes and followed her to the kitchens at the front of the Shelter, where the older woman slowly lowered herself onto an empty stool close to the breakfast fire. Amaya remained standing—she was already warm enough this day.

A few seconds later, she found she couldn't contain herself. "*What* are we supposed to do with that horrible man?"

Vasha shrugged. "I have no real answer for that, my dear, and I am truly sorry for it. In all of Osto's history, we never housed a person who was so . . . so singularly dangerous to us all."

"What, never?" Amaya frowned. Vasha wasn't quite the oldest person in the village, but she was the one who had lived here the longest.

"Never. Mostly, if people find they have no taste for our life here, they strike out on their own. Or sometimes they were problems that solved themselves." Vasha grinned. "If the kid isn't making sure every chicken gets in at night, you send him out on the wolf hunt. Problem solved."

"Vasha!" Amaya's voice rose in shock. "You never—"

"Oh, no, not alone, of course," Vasha waved off her horror. "I'm just saying, people are a lot more respectful of the rules if they get an up-close look at why the rules exist, that's all. Real close. Big teeth."

". . . ah," Amaya managed. She found a watery smile. "So, what's the house arrest supposed to be teaching Jon Newsome?"

"Oh, nothing," Vasha grimaced. "He's beyond learning. We mostly just wanted to keep him from talking with any of the newcomers. The peace was new and delicate, and it wouldn't have taken too many of his agitations for some of Drake's lieutenants to start having second thoughts."

"I think that's still a real concern," Amaya replied, frowning.

Vasha shook her head. "I don't. They're committed now, every last one of them. They've built here, they've struggled through the winter, and they're looking forward to their first summer's harvest in a real home. I think they're all coming along nicely."

"Maybe some more than others," Amaya allowed.

Some of the newcomers had certainly settled into the Oston way of life as though it were a calling they'd been waiting all their lives to answer. The armorer George had ensconced himself at Ahmed's expanded workbench almost instantly, and Devra had all but claimed the lieutenant Deetz as her partner as soon as the midnight election had been counted. Drake's former captain, Sirks, had thrown himself into every aspect of the village that would take him—he trained with the patrols, scavenged with the hunters, and worked the construction crews without complaint. But it was the quiet nights when he joined the Johnsons for dinner in their allotment, and Anton would show him the progress he'd made with his healing hand, that most reassured Amaya that maybe, just maybe, this would all work out.

Maybe.

DAY 2

t was a right mess, was what it was. Stan stood in the wreck of the house he'd thought he was building for the Blys and their children and found that, for the first time, he was glad Amaya and Cedric had never moved in.

The former Newsome house was little more than a pile of twisted nails and broken beams. Scraps of ancient plaster and newer clay covered the floor in a fine blanket. Skeletons of the walls still stood, a few even with stretches of intact material—enough to still be considered walls, at least. Across the fire-damaged living room, through a lonely, freestanding door frame, Stan spotted the stove he'd built himself. Scavenged bricks and hard-packed clay, with a tall, straight chimney leading to a roof that wasn't there anymore. It was the only part of the house that had survived the quake untouched.

Stan tried to tamp down on the spark of pride that gave him.

All the outlier buildings had suffered some damage during the quake, but the Newsome place had fared the worst. It wasn't too much of a surprise—it was the newest of the refurbished buildings, rebuilt only two and a half years ago. It had also been the first done without the supervision of Ravi Chandra, Vasha's father and the village's first leader. He had been an expert builder in his day and had led the reconstruction of the other outbuildings. After his passing, no one in Osto had even thought about adding more buildings until the Blys requested it. And, well, now they were seeing how that worked out.

But the stove still stood. It wasn't even the origin of the fire that had destroyed whatever the quake had left. The original frame of the building was strong, as were a few of the walls. It wasn't really any worse off than it had been before the restoration.

It wasn't any better, either.

Idly, Stan found himself wondering if his son Anton would be interested in helping to rebuild the place. Anton hadn't been interested in much lately, not since his injury on the day the newcomers had arrived. He had been a weaver, one of the most gifted artisans in the village, but since he'd lost the full use of his hand, he'd shown little interest in much of anything. Being reminded of the loss seemed to hurt him, but maybe something as basic and necessary as construction could be different enough, while still fanning that spark of creation—

"Hey, boss. You need to see this." Redbane, one of the newcomers, picked his way through the rubble. He was a big man, as most of them were, but he'd gone a bit soft around the middle—the sign of a man with a new profession that wasn't focused purely on physical strength. Stan smiled slightly as he approached. Redbane had volunteered for this job when he'd heard the announcement— apparently, he'd been one of the head builders of Esteben's Men before they came to Osto.

He carried a sour expression and a burlap bag that swelled as though full.

"There was a room in the back—it looks like it used to be pretty big. And it's full of boxes and bags and things like this."

Redbane held the bag out, and Stan took it and opened it.

His face darkened.

It was nearly full of turnips, large and blush pink, carefully trimmed of their greens and packed with sand and sawdust.

"No way these grew already. They were stored over winter," Stan muttered. "How much was there?"

Redbane jerked his head toward the back of the building. "You'd better come see."

———

"Turnips, potatoes, carrots, onions—"

Amaya caught her breath as she leaned against the kitchen counters. "Real onions? We don't even have those!"

"We used to, but we had a mite problem four years ago that wiped them all out."

"Do you think they've been keeping them since then?"

Stan narrowed his eyes in thought. "No, I don't think they last that long. But they may have grown them somewhere in secret. Or traded for them from someone passing by and decided not to share."

"That's . . ." *Incredibly selfish,* she thought. But at least not outright theft from the village.

"There's more," Stan said. "Building materials. Nails, boards, fabric. Candles. Oil. Enough to make a difference. Enough to have kept more people warm last winter."

His weathered face was grim, his eyes narrow. Amaya could only imagine that she looked the same. Osto didn't have much in the way of crime, but there was one thing that every Oston abhorred above all: the selfish act of hoarding necessities for yourself. And this past winter had been a thin one, with the unexpected population increase. Supplies such as these would have helped immensely. Until now, the Newsomes, as a family, had been difficult and deeply unlikeable, but they'd never been actively working against the community.

Or at least, Amaya corrected herself, they'd never been caught. It sounded like they'd been hoarding food for a while now. And still claiming their full share from Oston supplies.

She frowned down at the bag of turnips, then picked one out and gave it a careful inspection. It was larger than what normally grew in Oston fields and an attractive light pink color that she hadn't seen before.

"Do you think they traded for these or grew them?"

"Ma'am?"

Amaya shook her head. "It makes a difference, doesn't it? Are they trading for these somehow? Or do they have a secret field somewhere that they aren't sharing? Because if they're just trading . . ."

If they were just trading, she could let it go. If they were trading their own supplies or their own share of Oston goods for different varieties and different crops, she could forgive it. But if they were, in fact, growing their own food, using their labor for themselves apart from the village, and still taking as much from the village supply as everyone else . . . If they'd had so much that village children wouldn't have had to go hungry or cold . . .

That would be a crime. That would be unforgivable. Something would have to be done about it—*she'd* have to do something about it, as Headwoman. As much as she disliked Jon Newsome, she couldn't see that going well in any way.

Two years ago, she and Cedric had requested the village's help to move their growing family to an outlying building. Enough people had agreed that Vasha had arranged a full new work rotation to refurbish one of the ruins outside town. It had been a heady, exciting time, a joyful time, one that had finally made her feel like she'd truly been accepted into this place she'd come to call home.

Months later, just as the newly rebuilt house was ready for the Blys to move in, the Newsomes had convened a village meeting to contest the Blys' right to move into the new building. It had been an ugly fight. The people who had helped rebuild the outlier had thought they were specifically helping the Blys and their children, and some went so far as to say they wouldn't have done the same for the Newsomes. Words were said that had not been taken back to this day. Amaya and Cedric finally conceded in the interest of keeping the village peaceful. But what was past was not forgotten and certainly not forgiven. Jonathan Newsome had never seemed the least bit sorry for his actions, and Amaya had quietly nursed the wound he'd dealt her family ever since.

She'd been secretly glad to see Jon's downfall last year with the collapse of his own machinations, and she'd been very, very glad that it wasn't up to her to decide the punishment of the man who'd tried to kill her son. Befriending Sarah and welcoming Gabrielle into her family had helped her accept that the whole Newsome family wasn't completely loathsome, even if the patriarch himself was vile. And what she'd learned from Sarah suggested that many of the residents of the Newsome house were looking for a way out. That nuance, and Vasha's cautious sentencing of Jon to house arrest, had been . . . enough. It had been healing.

But this? This was evidence that the whole family had been complicit in an ongoing crime against the entire village. Including her friend Sarah and her new daughter-in-law—they had both known, presumably for years, and never told a soul. They had both chosen to protect Jon over the village, even as everyone went hungry and children shivered with cold.

And the village's leader was in charge of making it right.

Why had she ever agreed to be Headwoman?

"Ma'am?"

Amaya took a deep breath, feeling her shoulders shudder. "Gather up everything that's still usable. Food, supplies, whatever you find. Anything that isn't personal goes into the village's supplies."

Stan nodded. "And the Newsomes?"

Amaya shook her head, staring at the turnip. "I don't know. We can't punish the whole family."

"But you can put up Jon in a room on his own."

This was Danica, who stood just inside the Shelter's main door, still squinting as she waited for her eyes to adjust. She was a tall woman in no-nonsense trousers and a long, undyed tunic. She wore a purple spring flower tucked above one ear, somewhat incongruously.

"I'm sorry?"

Danica approached and hooked a stool over to her, perching on it with one leg bent at an odd angle. "Jon Newsome. You've got him in Vasha's room, right? That's why she spent the night with us."

Amaya nodded. "And we are very grateful you were able to accommodate her—"

"We?" Danica quirked an eyebrow. "If you're speaking for yourself, just say so."

Amaya flushed, angry without really knowing why. "Vasha volunteered her room herself. It was the most logical solution. And it's only temporary."

"Until *we* get their house rebuilt, you mean?" Danica shook her head. "I know Lani and I are relatively new here, but we heard what they did to you. Seems to me having that house collapse was some sort of— what's the word? Fate, maybe?"

Amaya had been trying to avoid such thoughts. "It could just as easily have been someone else living there. Earthquakes aren't exactly divine punishments."

"But it wasn't." Danica reached over and picked up the turnip bag. She glanced inside and snorted. "We've all heard the rumors about them, and it turns out they're true. Now you're what, going to reward them by rebuilding their stolen home?"

She hadn't even thought that far ahead. "I don't know yet. I need . . . I need more information before we decide on anything."

"Before *you* decide on anything."

Amaya shook her head firmly at that. "I'm not going to lead like that. I was elected because people trust me to be fair. I'm going to get the facts first, hear from everyone involved, and get advice. Anything that comes from this will be . . . the decision of the whole village."

"Hm." Danica gave her a strange, side-angled look and plopped the bag of turnips back on the counter. "That sounds good. It also sounds like it will take time. Time in which that asshole is sleeping in Vasha's bed."

A brief flash of mischief prompted Amaya to ask, "Would you rather be hosting Jon Newsome?"

Danica gave a full-body shudder. "Not for all the turnips in the world."

Ahmed was surprised at his own relief to see finally the blunt grey block of the Shelter rise across the fields. It hadn't been all that long of a journey—three days, all told—but it was the longest he'd been away from Osto since his grandmother had brought him there as a small child. Even the winter's new construction around the edges, the short, squat buildings encroaching on once-open space, seemed familiar and welcoming in a way he never would have expected when they'd set out. The newcomers' horses grazed peacefully outside the new barn, and sheep clustered in the farthest possible corner of their enclosure away from the monstrous beasts. In the fields, farmers bent to the task of sowing and planting their stored grain. Ahmed didn't know much about farming, but there had to be a faster way to plant a field. Individuals with hoes and shovels seemed so primitive, somehow. There must have been better ways to do it once. Maybe that would be his next project—

"Ho! George! Ahmed! Back already? How was the trip?" The speaker was Deetz, one of the former raiders. He had settled in faster than most and usually spent his time minding the animals with his partner, Devra. His easygoing, if slow, nature made him one of the more likable newcomers, so far as Ahmed was concerned.

George pulled his horse to heel. "Ho, Deetz. More surprising than we expected. How did things go here?"

Deetz gently pushed away the nose of a friendly mare and hopped the fence out of the horse paddock. He extended his hand to Ahmed's mount as he approached and gently stroked her cheeks when she gave a familiar whuffle.

"Had an earthquake. You felt it?"

"We did." George stood up in his stirrups and peered at the village beyond. "How bad was it here?"

"Bad." Deetz paused, and gave Ahmed a canny look. "Shelter's okay. Outliers took some damage. Newsome house is flattened."

Ahmed's stomach clenched at the mention of the place. He knew the reason for Deetz's hesitation—since the Newsomes had attempted to kidnap him last summer, no one seemed to want to discuss the family around him. He'd noticed that he never seemed to share a work shift with any of them, and he'd caught people's pauses and the hitches in their voices as they realized who they were talking to about what. He wasn't completely oblivious—the fact that he was kept separate from the family that formed nearly ten percent of Osto's population was hard to miss.

It made him appreciate Deetz's bluntness all the more.

"Flattened? What are they doing now?" George seemed to be processing the news faster than he was.

Deetz shrugged. "Rebuilding. Some of them are camping while they build."

There was a pause. When he spoke, George used a too-casual tone that Ahmed had come to realize meant he was hiding some deeper feeling. "And Jon?"

Deetz shrugged. "Dunno. Ask Amaya."

George nodded, and a moment passed before he said, "I think we'll do just that. We need to see her anyway."

Deetz waved back at the Shelter. "Kitchens, last I saw."

"Thanks."

Deetz gave Ahmed's horse another pat on the neck before he stepped back. Ahmed nodded at him, unsure what else to say, and the two of them rode on.

George led them up to the Shelter door, where he easily dismounted and hitched his horse to a newly built rail. When he finished, he came around the side of Ahmed's horse and knitted his fingers together into a makeshift step. Though he didn't say a word, Ahmed winced in embarrassment. He managed a mumbled "thank you" as he dismounted with one foot in George's hands and a hand for balance on his shoulder. Even with the help, it was still a clumsy affair. George only shrugged and flipped the reins, tying the second horse to the rail without a word.

"What are we going to tell them?" Ahmed asked, once he was sure both feet were on the ground.

George blinked. "The truth, right?"

"Yeah, I mean . . ." What did he mean? Ahmed was less capable with words than he was with gadgets. And though he'd been perfectly comfortable speaking his mind with Vasha, the new Headwoman always seemed too busy to make much time for him. She certainly appreciated his contributions to Osto, but her appreciation was much less personal than Vasha's unflagging support.

"I'll do the talking," George said. He reached out and tousled Ahmed's hair, a familiarity he wouldn't have tolerated from anyone else in the world. "You can chime in whenever you're comfortable, okay?"

Ahmed flushed, embarrassed by how grateful he was at the reprieve. ". . . okay."

Inside, they found Amaya in the kitchens as predicted, along with Stan and Danica, all gathered around a lumpy brown sack on the counter. The three of them looked grim enough already that Ahmed found himself casting longing looks at his workbench in the far corner, but he wasn't about to abandon George entirely to this duty.

Amaya noticed them first. "You're back! That was . . . that's fast, isn't it? We weren't expecting you at least until tomorrow." Then, half a second later, "Was it the quake?"

George gave a grim smile. Never one to drag out a conversation, he said, "No, actually. It was the village we found at the river."

"What?!" That was Stan and Danica both.

Amaya seemed to take a long second, tapping the fingers of one hand on the counter. "A village?"

"Of a sort." George nodded. "Not like Osto. No old buildings. Looked like mostly tents and wagons. A few new wooden homes. Small."

"How many people? Were they at your waterfall?"

"Wagons?" Danica asked, her eyes wide.

George nodded at the questions. "We didn't get a good look. Tried to stay hidden. Pretty sure they didn't see us. But . . . maybe fifty?"

"Wagons and new buildings," Danica said, leaning forward over the counter. "So, they haven't been there long. Where do you think they came from?"

"And do they know about us?" Stan was frowning, clearly already running through the worst possible scenarios.

"Dunno," George said.

"I'd think they'd come say hi, if they did." Amaya was frowning.

"Do you think they arrived in the winter? Or could they have just come this spring?"

George and Ahmed exchanged glances. Ahmed racked his brain, trying to remember any details that might give them the answers they were looking for. One thing stood out.

"They had fish traps in the river," Ahmed said. "Big circular ones, built of wood that didn't look a season weathered. And flags . . ." His eyes widened. "Really bright colors! They must have dyes that we don't."

"And they weren't faded at all." George nodded in agreement. "So, they came from somewhere with different plants and haven't been here long."

"Can it just be coincidence, that they're so close?" Amaya was staring down at the brown sack with a strange expression.

George shrugged. "The west is getting worse. Hotter, drier, more fires than before. If we left, makes sense others are, too. And Osto is . . . famous."

"And that makes us a target," Amaya breathed. It was impossible to ignore the truth in her words. George had to know that better than anyone else present.

"They . . . they didn't look like raiders," Ahmed volunteered. "Just people. People who wanted to fish."

"Trying to provide for themselves," Amaya nodded. "That's a good sign. But it doesn't mean they won't want what we have once they see us."

George was quiet at that. All of them were.

"If they keep to themselves, there shouldn't be any problem," Stan volunteered. "Maybe we just leave them alone?"

"We're going to meet each other eventually," Danica said, frowning. "Wouldn't it be better if it's on our terms?"

Amaya nodded. "What are you suggesting?"

Danica waved at George and then back out the open door, where the two tied-up horses could be seen grazing. "We can take care of ourselves, right? Wasn't that part of the point of allowing the Men to join? So they could protect us against other attacks? Well, here's one now."

"They haven't attacked!" Ahmed said, and George frowned darkly.

"And maybe they'll be less likely to if fifty of you guys and your guns and horses show up and introduce yourselves." Danica crossed her arms and leaned back. "Nothing wrong with showing our strength."

"We're not asking the newcomers to do that," Amaya said, her voice suddenly soft. "That's not why they're here. That's not the Oston way."

"And what is the Oston way? Treating our criminals with kid gloves and inviting the invaders right on in?"

"Hey!" Ahmed was by no means the least surprised person at the table at his own outburst. But he couldn't stand hearing anyone insult George or Vasha like that. "Vasha was right. The Men proved it in the election. They're here because they *don't* want to be invaders anymore. And you can't force them to be!"

"I'm not trying to force them. I'm saying this is a chance for them to use their strength to help us rather than just eating us out of all our stores!"

"They *are* helping us!"

"George is helping," Danica said, nodding at the big man. "What about the rest of them?"

"That's not—"

"Stop it!" Amaya slammed her hands down on the counter, producing a noise so loud that Ahmed flinched back, certain she must have hurt herself. "We're not going over there like invaders ourselves. And we're not treating the newcomers any differently than anyone else in the village. So long as they're here, they're Ostons, not just soldiers."

"So . . ." Stan raised his eyebrows. "What *are* we going to do?"

There was a long pause, and Amaya narrowed her eyes.

"I think . . . we need a clearer idea of what their intentions are," Amaya said. "And I think we need to talk to someone who's handled situations like this before."

With this declaration, the Headwoman sounded certain of herself for the first time since they'd arrived.

———

The walk to Lani and Danica's cottage was an easy one, though not often traveled. None of Osto's outlying buildings were particularly far from the Shelter, but most of them followed the single cracked and broken road that ran north from the Shelter itself to the crop fields. The ruins there had been thoroughly picked clean for decades, and anything useable was repurposed into the Shelter, along with the few structures worth saving. When they'd first arrived, Lani and Danica had instead opted to build themselves a new place entirely, making a first foray into taming the forests south of the Shelter. They had found a natural clearing a short walk into the woods, cleared the brush and widened it, and built a small one-room cottage amongst the trees. They were adamant that visitors were always welcome, and they were very much a part of everyday village life, but the simple fact of their removal and the extra effort it took to visit them meant that they enjoyed a certain amount of quiet and privacy no one else in the village could hope for. From what Lani had said about her previous life in an autocratic enclave, where every aspect of a person's life was under strict control and surveillance, the peace and freedom of the cottage was a healing balm on two fatigued souls.

Amaya had only made the trek herself a few times before, and it had been long enough that she could mark the signs of the changing seasons since her last visit. Green fuzzed the trees, a soft portent of the solid canopy that would develop in only a few weeks' time. Determined early plants speared up through the leaf loam, teasing the lush displays of leaves or flowers soon to come. One spectacular tree seemed to bow under clouds of early white flowers, and as she approached it, she could hear the buzzing of what had to be hundreds of bees flitting through the myriad petals.

The cottage was a simple thing—four walls and a roof that sloped down in a single plane of wooden boards, long eaves overhanging the front door. A low fence of scavenged timber ringed the building, serving mostly as a trellis for the anticipated profusion of the garden. Further back, set almost into the forest, she could see the cornet of a beehive, Danica's pride and joy. The entire scene teemed with the renewed stirrings of life, the living heartbeat of the forest slowly awakening after a long winter's slumber.

Amaya appreciated the quiet beauty of the view, but a part of her still shuddered quietly at the perceived isolation, the loss of the security brought by the constant noise and presence of humanity.

A cry broke through the quiet of the forest, and Amaya grinned. Maybe they had enough noise out here, after all.

Chloe's head peered around the doorframe, followed quickly by her pudgy body. The girl had a full head of black curls, clearly inherited from her mother, Lani, and wide dark eyes that either woman could have claimed. She crawled fast, faster than one would expect, down the path from the door. Maybe that fence served more than one purpose, after all.

"Get back here, child." Vasha's voice was a welcome counterpoint to the baby's cry, calm and rich and full of good humor. Amaya found herself smiling as she pushed open the gate, a wash of relief flooding her for the first time since the quake had hit the day before.

"How are you finding it, Vasha?" she asked.

The walk from the gate to the cottage door was lined with carefully tended beds of dark black loam, orderly rectangles dotted with small sticks that must mark the location of future growth. Amaya found her thoughts drawn back to the Newsomes and their hoarding, drawing unwelcome parallels between the small garden and the suspected secret crop field.

It wasn't the same. It couldn't be. But the thought was enough to darken her pleasure at seeing Vasha whole and hale in the doorway, hefting Chloe onto a hip.

"Amaya, welcome! Come on in!" That voice belonged to Lani, far enough back in the dimness of the cottage that Amaya couldn't see her yet.

Vasha turned aside, keeping a firm hold on the squirming child, and ushered Amaya inside before closing the door after her.

The cottage's interior was bursting with the evidence of Lani and Danica's industry. Though the place was small, they had sectioned off separate areas for sleeping, food preparation, and general living. Though perhaps it was more accurate to call the last a workshop, as the walls were lined with shelves of sealed clay pots, tiny planters with pale, delicate seedlings, and hanging bunches of dried herbs and flowers. Amaya thought again of the Newsomes and their hoard, squirreled away in the dark of a home to which they never invited anyone.

Lani was busying herself at a work surface, carefully arranging several small clay plates on a larger wooden tray.

"You're just in time," Vasha was saying. "Lani was telling me about her efforts to flavor last year's honey, and we're going to sample some."

"Won't you join us?" Lani turned at last, the heavy tray carefully held in both hands. Her smile was bright and completely guileless, and Amaya immediately felt guilty for her dark thoughts. Danica and Lani weren't like that. They were true Ostons, through and through.

"I'd love to, thank you."

Lani placed the tray on the one small table in the living area as Vasha did her best to hold on to an increasingly squirmy Chloe. Once the food was safe, Vasha set the girl down next to her mother. She stayed where she was put, blinking around at the visitors. Lani scooped a quantity of honey from one plate with a blunt serving paddle and offered it to Chloe, who immediately seized her hand and pulled it to her mouth, smearing her cheeks with thick, gooey honey.

"Please, help yourselves," Lani said to Amaya and Vasha. "The bread's just from Osto, but this is the first time I've opened these flavored batches. This is plain." She held up the paddle she'd offered Chloe, then pointed in turn at each of the other three plates. "And there's rosemary, elderberry, and dandelion."

"Dandelion?" Amaya asked.

Lani shrugged. "Like I said, it's an experiment. I know it's edible, but I don't know if it will infuse at all."

"We used to eat a lot of dandelions in Osto, before we got the crop fields to the size they are," Vasha observed. "I thought I'd never have to eat them again."

"Oh," Lani said, her face suddenly darkening in a frown. "I . . ."

Vasha grinned and waved it off. "I also never thought we'd have anything so sweet." She lathered a generous dollop of the dandelion honey onto a bread slice and bit into it with every sign of enjoyment.

Amaya decided discretion was the better part of not dying from a plant she'd never heard of and chose the rosemary honey. She scraped a thin layer of it over a slice, gave a quiet nod of thanks to Lani, and bit in.

The resulting taste riveted her to her chair and tingled down her spine. Sweetness like she had never experienced coated her lips, her tongue, her mouth. The taste seemed to jolt her mind awake and catch her breath, and she swore her heart skipped a beat in surprise and recognition of this one taste, this one sensation that she had been missing so much in her life. For a moment, all thought fled from her head as she found herself centered in her body, focused on a single physical reaction. She sucked at her lips, determined not to waste a single bit of the golden treasure. Somehow, the very bones of her teeth hurt, but she couldn't bring herself to care.

". . . oh," Amaya breathed.

"That's the rosemary," Lani said, nodding in satisfaction. "I knew that one would work."

It wasn't the rosemary that was making her feel this way. Amaya frowned, trying to figure out how Vasha and Lani could both be sitting there, munching on bread and honey and chatting calmly. Amaya felt more akin to Chloe in that moment, who couldn't seem to stop herself from wiggling in her seat.

She blinked, realizing Lani had asked her a question. "Oh. I'm sorry. What were you saying?"

Lani smiled and tilted her head in amusement. "I said, 'What brings you here today?'"

"Ah, right." Amaya forced her thoughts back to her purpose. "Actually, I came to talk to Vasha. If . . . if you don't mind. I was hoping to seek her advice."

"Oh, of course!" Lani waved an airy hand. "Important village stuff. I understand. Do you need the munchkin and I to give you privacy?"

"Oh, no. At least, I don't think so." Amaya watched Vasha for any clue about how to handle this, but she simply shrugged and took another bite.

Well. Fine. Vasha had always been open about her rulings, and Amaya would be, too. "Please, stay. Though it might be a bit boring for the little one."

"Oh, don't worry about her," Lani said brightly. "She doesn't really have a choice."

"Right . . ." Amaya nibbled at her bread. The smaller bite was much more manageable than the first had been. Though the sweetness was still an overwhelming surge of flavor, she was better prepared for it and kept her composure as she chewed and swallowed.

"Is it internal or external?" Vasha asked, a canny look in her eye.

Amaya gave a bark of laughter. "Both. It's both."

"Ah." Vasha leaned forward. "Let's start with the internal. What has Newsome done now?"

"By Allah." Amaya almost hung her head in her hands. "It's not just one Newsome. It's all of them."

"All?" Lani asked, her voice squeaking. "Even Sarah?"

Amaya nodded in confirmation. "All. Even Sarah. Even Gabrielle. We've found they were hoarding supplies. Food, materials, things we all could have used. Enough to have made a difference last year."

Lani drew a breath, sucking at her teeth. "And you're certain Sarah knew?"

"I . . . haven't talked to her. But Stan said it's been happening at least since last year's harvest. She had to know."

"And food, too?"

Amaya nodded again. "I saw it myself. They had turnips that we don't grow here. And Stan said there was more. A lot more."

Vasha nodded to herself. "So, a hidden field. I thought so."

"You *thought* so?" Amaya heard her voice go loud, and worked to regain composure. "Why didn't you say anything?"

"I had no evidence." Vasha shrugged. "What was there to say? 'I think the people that stole your house might still be stealing?' What good would that do? With no evidence to back it up? You already knew to watch them."

"I . . ." Amaya paused at that. She was right. The Newsome family had been a known problem for a long time: insular, thuggish, and ruled by a fool who thought himself a king. They'd already been widely disliked before the events of last year, and after the failed takeover, many of the family had been all but shunned by residents of the Shelter. Exceptions were made for Sarah and her two youngest children, who had very visibly chosen the Osto community over family, but overall it was not hard to believe the worst of the Newsomes.

The fact that she'd been so ready to condemn her friend without even talking to her signaled just how deep the prejudice ran, how ingrained the reaction was. Amaya frowned to herself, recognizing an ugliness she did not like.

"Being a leader is hard enough," Vasha said, the lines in her face deepening as she spoke. "You have to strive to be even-handed with all your people without letting your moods blow you one way today, the next tomorrow. You can't let your biases lead you to treat anyone differently—not your friends or the pains in your ass."

"I thought Sarah *was* my friend," Amaya said. It was dangerously close to the true cause of the sinking feeling in her stomach.

"She is, as best she knows how to be." Vasha took another bite of her bread and honey. "She's also trying to figure out how to be . . . how to exist outside the world Jonathan built. She spent years under his thumb, listening to his poison. She's only been free of him for a few months. Give it time."

Amaya bit her lip at that. She and Cedric had essentially taken in Sarah and her children, setting them up in a family allotment right next to theirs. They ate their evening meal together and talked nearly everyday, about anything and everything.

Or not everything, she realized now. Sarah had never brought up Jon or her life in the outlier house. Gabrielle rarely did, and even Eric would only sometimes mention that he missed one or another of his brothers. The three of them were oddly silent on the subject of their former family and abode. That silence didn't have to mean collusion.

Amaya hung her head, staring at the tray of bread and honey, as she quietly reassessed her own thoughts and her interpretation of Sarah and her children. She'd thought they were doing well, fine on their own once they'd left their toxic home. But people were more fragile than that, and healing deep wounds took time—especially when those wounds were to the mind rather than the body.

She sighed deeply. "You are . . . you are right. Sarah is not to blame. Only Jon. And I still don't know what to do with him!"

"Do?" Lani blinked. "You're not going to keep him under house arrest?"

"That clearly isn't helping anything," Amaya said. "It's just allowing him to stay out of sight and skip out on duty rotations."

"Hm." Vasha gave a grunt of acknowledgment. "I had rather hoped he'd have a change of heart and beg to come back by now."

"What has Osto done before with . . . with criminals?"

Vasha gave a snort. "We haven't had any for so long as I've been here. Before . . . I think the main punishment was exile."

"Exile? Like just sending him away?" Amaya's eyes widened. "He's an old man, Vasha! He'd die out there!"

"Yes, thank you for the reminder," Vasha said, an edge to her tone. "I said that's what we *used* to do. I never did."

"It's hardly in line with Oston values," Lani said quietly, and Amaya had to agree.

"But then, what *would* be in line with Oston values? We can't bring him back in; he's clearly too dangerous. Especially with the newcomers still unsettled and the winter so bad. He would . . ." Amaya shook her head. "He would see it as weakness."

The other women were quiet at that, each seeing the truth in the words.

Chloe was the one to break it. She reached for the stack of bread slices, overbalanced, and pitched forward with a cry. Lani caught her easily and set her upright again with soft admonishments. She took the opportunity to wipe the child's mouth, then started fussing with her shirt.

"What else?" Vasha asked.

"Hm?" Amaya had to wrench her gaze away from the child.

"You said there was something else. Something external. What?"

"Oh!" Amaya gave a rueful smile. "George and Ahmed have found another village. Neighbors, almost. A day and a half away on horseback."

"Oh, what are they like?" Lani asked.

At the same time, Vasha raised an eyebrow. "And?"

Amaya paused. "And . . . we aren't sure how to approach them."

Vasha closed her eyes. She took a long moment, then nodded. "Amaya," she said softly. "I won't always be here to guide you."

The words were strangely cold inside her. Amaya stared, feeling the truth as something hard and foreign in her throat, something that ought to remain unspoken. She couldn't imagine Osto without Vasha.

"I . . . I know."

The silence stretched between them before Vasha gave a deep sigh. "But I am here now, so I will do what I can. Do tell. What are they like?"

"They . . ." Amaya paused, giving Vasha a close look. Was that it? Were they just going to move on without discussing that statement any further?

Maybe it was better that way.

Maybe some things were better left unsaid.

She sighed, and repeated everything George and Ahmed had told her about the camp by the river. The tents, the wagons, the few completed structures. The fish weirs. The flags. The children.

"How many?" Vasha asked, once Amaya had finished her summary.

"They said they didn't get a good look. Maybe fifty to seventy-five?"

Vasha nodded. "Too many to invite in here right now, anyway. Maybe in a few years."

That hadn't even occurred to her. Amaya's eyes widened as she considered the complications of yet another influx of population. "We're already stretched with the newcomers—"

"I know, that's why I said so," Vasha replied. She waved a hand. "So, we leave them where they are, if it's where they seem to want to be."

"They aren't too close?" Lani asked.

Vasha snorted. "Too close? They're a day beyond even our longest patrol route. They've obviously been there already for a while. We might never have even found them if it weren't for Ahmed's wild ideas."

Amaya nodded. "But . . . we do have to do something. Let them know we know about them."

"Seems logical," Vasha agreed. "Send them . . . a delegation, I think that's what to call it."

"Find out if they're friendly," Lani added.

"And let them know we can defend ourselves if they ain't," Vasha finished. "Maybe some of our best talkers backed by some of the scariest newcomers." She paused. "And George. Everyone likes George."

Amaya couldn't help but laugh at that. "Everyone does like George."

"There you go. One thing I can help you with." Vasha smiled and reached over to pat Amaya's hand. "And you let me know how it goes, you hear? It would be good to expand our world a bit."

Amaya managed a weak smile at that. It wasn't everything she'd been looking for when she came, but it was a start. The beginnings of a plan. A direction. It felt good to have a direction on *something*, at least.

———

Sarah stepped back and surveyed her small infirmary. She nodded to herself, satisfied: restocked, cleaned, organized, everything in its place. She was ready for the spring planting season.

More than winter, more than fall, spring was what she privately thought of as her busy season. The village, cooped up all winter, flexed disused muscles after too long sitting idle and crouching over small projects; she had learned early on to stock up on ache soothers and pain-relieving teas. It was a struggle to keep the stores intact over winter, but it always paid off when planting came around.

She flicked a wrinkle out of the top layer of her stack of linen bandages and closed the box, protecting them from dust and anything else that might be floating about. Never a fan of an idle moment, she then picked up her current knitting project—a square of dull green wool she vaguely intended to turn into a blanket—and sat down to enjoy the silence.

It didn't last long. Footsteps approached the infirmary and hesitated at the threshold. Sarah looked up, alert, as the heavy door slowly swung inward. A dark blonde head poked around it, and Sarah instantly tensed up.

"Gabrielle! Are you okay? What's wrong?"

On hearing her name, her daughter pushed the door the rest of the way open and came inside. She quickly gave the small room a once-over, as though ensuring they were alone, and closed the door behind her.

"Hi, Mom."

Sarah caught the sardonic edge and managed a wan smile. "Hi, heart. Are you okay?"

". . . yes," Gabrielle said. She trailed in, her steps strangely hesitant. Her eyes still darted around the room, looking at everything but her mother.

Sarah hesitated. "Is it Umair, then?"

"No! No, he's fine. Everyone's . . . everyone's fine, mom."

She caught her breath and forced herself to breathe slowly, counting as she'd learned to calm herself. "Everyone" included her ex-husband, her sons, and everyone else in the village. Which meant that whatever was bothering Gabrielle wasn't a medical issue.

"Okay. Have a seat, heart. Should I make us some tea?"

"That . . . yes. Tea would be good." There was a beat before she added, "Lavender?"

"I think I have some," Sarah answered, managing a smile. "Will you light the fire?"

Lavender had always been Gabrielle's favorite, but since they'd moved into the village, they'd been eating from the communal kitchens, which had only served barley tea all winter.

A few minutes later, they sat with two clay mugs and a pot full of steaming water, slowly infusing with small purple flowers. Gabrielle leaned over the teapot and inhaled deeply. For the first time since she'd arrived, her shoulders dropped, and Sarah realized exactly how tense the girl had been.

"Dear heart—" she said, and stopped. Gabrielle would speak in her own time.

"Mama, you like the Blys, right? You like Umair?"

"Of course," Sarah replied. She blinked. Gabrielle, of all people, should know she didn't need to ask that. But for good measure, she added, "Amaya and Cedric have been better friends than I could have ever asked for."

"Right," Gabrielle said. And a moment later, "And Umair?"

Sarah nodded. "Umair is a fine young man who makes you happy."

"Mom." Gabrielle frowned at that. "That doesn't mean you like him."

Sarah hesitated. "I don't know him the way you do. We've never really talked. We've never been alone in a room together. I can only judge him based on what he shows me and how he makes you feel."

Gabrielle nodded at that and was quiet for a moment. "You were . . . okay with the two of us leaving together."

Sarah felt a shudder go down her back at the memory. It had been a harrowing conversation in the middle of the night. She'd been barely awake, terrified that Jon would interrupt, and for once, she went with her first instincts rather than letting her fear overpower her. "I thought anything had to be better than where we were."

"You were right," Gabrielle said fiercely. "But I'm glad it didn't come to that in the end."

Sarah smiled. "Me too, dear heart. Me, too."

The silence fell again, and Sarah gave the tea a stir. She thought it looked about the right color, so she stretched a tea cloth across the pot's spout and carefully poured servings into the waiting mugs. The aroma bloomed throughout the room, and both women took deep breaths and let out small sighs of pleasure.

"Thanks, Mom." Gabrielle took the mug proffered and blew across the surface.

"Of course."

Gabrielle stared down into her mug, then looked up and watched Sarah take a tentative sip. She was clearly struggling with something, but didn't seem prepared to say much else.

Sarah decided to take a leap. "Are you . . . thinking about getting married?"

"Married?!" The idea was apparently so surprising that Gabrielle put her mug down with more than necessary force. "What? Mom, no one gets married anymore!"

"Well . . ." *Your father and I did.* But that was not exactly a persuasive argument. "You could, you know. If you wanted to."

"I don't want to!"

"I'm just saying—"

"No, Mom, that's not it!"

"Then what is it? You're clearly upset. Tell me what's going on."

Gabrielle hunched her shoulders, then seemed to catch herself and straightened up, a decision made.

"Mom, I'm—I'm pregnant."

Sarah did not drop her mug, and later, when she had a moment, she'd be very glad for that fact.

"Pregnant!" She blinked. "You're—you're going to be a mother!"

Gabrielle nodded. "And Umair's going to be a father. And . . . Pa's going to be . . ."

". . . furious," Sarah finished for her. Her eyes widened at the thought. Gabrielle's hesitation suddenly made much more sense to her. "Oh, dear heart. Don't let that dampen your joy. This is so exciting!"

"Is it? Mom . . ." Gabrielle stared down at her mug again. "It's not just Pa. I just keep thinking about being a child. About how hard things were. How dangerous. How there was never enough food. This last winter . . ."

Sarah shook her head firmly. "It won't be like that for you. We're in the Shelter now. You'll have all of Osto to help. You've seen how everyone cares for Chloe. You'll have that."

"I suppose." Gabrielle shook her head. "But I also saw how scared Lani and Danica were last summer. How worried they were that the raiders might . . ."

Sarah nodded. "That . . . could have gone very badly," she agreed. "But it didn't. And now we have new friends and more help around the village. We'll be able to grow more food because of them, and defend ourselves against other raids. Things will only get better."

"That's what I keep telling myself," Gabrielle said softly. "I'm just . . . I'm scared, Mama. I'm so scared. Everyone says giving birth is so painful, and so many things go wrong. How did you do it so many times?"

"Ah . . ." Sarah gave a self-conscious laugh. "On the upside, you never remember how much it hurts until you're doing it again."

"Again!"

"Not that—I mean, it's your choice, dear heart."

"Is it!?" Gabrielle stood, no longer able to stay in one place as she processed. "It wasn't my choice to *get* pregnant! I thought we were keeping track! I mean—"

The girl looked wildly around. "Mama, I don't know what to *do!* We aren't ready!"

"Oh, Gaby . . ." Sarah stood as well, rounding the table to approach her daughter. When the girl didn't flinch away, she wrapped her in a hug. "It's okay. It will be okay. You'll see."

"You can't know that," Gabrielle said. She gave a deep sniff and buried her face in her mother's shoulder. "I just . . . I keep thinking of everything that can happen."

"You get that from me," Sarah said softly. "I'm sorry."

The silence, this time, was punctuated with strangled gasps as Gabrielle fought against her sobs. Sarah frowned—her heart ached for her child, but there seemed to be more than simple fear playing on Gabrielle's mind. She waited, certain it would come out in its own time.

"Mama, I just . . . what if I'm not ready?"

"Aw, sweetie. No one ever is." It felt like a platitude the second it left her mouth, but it was still the truest answer she had.

"Were you?"

"Ready to be a mother?" Sarah paused at that. There were too many complications in her reaction to that. Too many painful memories to hold up to the light and examine. "I was younger than you are now," she eventually managed.

"But were you *ready?*"

She should have known her clever daughter wouldn't let her get away with it. "Gaby, you can't compare your father and me to you and Umair. There's a world of difference."

"Umair's nothing like Pa!"

"He isn't," Sarah agreed quickly. "And thank goodness for that. He'll be a wonderful father."

"Oh, Mama," Gabrielle sniffed. "I just . . . I just wish I knew what to do. I wish I could *know* it was safe."

Sarah couldn't help herself; a harsh laugh escaped her at the plea. "That's one thing no one gets in this world, love."

Gabrielle was quiet for a long moment. "What if I can't do this?"

"Oh baby," Sarah whispered. Her heart broke for her daughter, her family, her whole fractured world. The world that turned what should have been a joyous time into one of fear and doubt. "You aren't doing it alone. You have me, and Umair, and everyone in Osto."

Her only answers were sobs as Gabrielle collapsed fully into her arms.

DAY 3

T he news of the new village had traveled faster than Amaya had even realized. She hadn't expected to keep it totally secret, but she hadn't expected this, either—her handpicked team, gathering to set off on their first diplomatic mission ever, found itself surrounded by villagers kitted out in their best coats and boots and determined to join the expedition. They filled the square in front of the Shelter, a hard-packed dirt surface surrounded by the winter's new construction.

"This is supposed to be a friendly visit!" Amaya called, raising her voice to be heard over the noise of the crowd. "Not an invasion! We can't show up with so many people if we want them to believe we're friendly!"

"Okay, but then why's *he* going?" someone called.

Technically, there was no indication of who "he" could be, but Amaya could guess.

"Everyone I've chosen is here for a reason! Not least of which is that they can be spared from the planting for a few days!"

That won her a few sullen glances from youngsters who'd thought they were getting out of their farming chores. Amaya glared back at them. Not even Cedric was coming. She'd kissed him and the children goodbye back in the lot, but now she wondered if it would have been a stronger statement to have him standing there to see her off.

"Look." Amaya lowered her voice, and was gratified to hear the noise of the crowd drop accordingly. It was something Vasha had taught her—shouting over a din only made more din. Speak quietly, and people would strain to hear. "Drake and the newcomers are coming to show strength. Sarah will look after any injuries along the way. Devra and Deetz are looking after the horses for those of us who don't know anything about them. Myself included."

She was gratified to hear a smattering of laughter at that.

"That's eight people already. We don't want to overwhelm them. We'll seem friendly, but strong. Please, trust me."

"And me? You have to take me." Ahmed stood at the edge of the crowd, holding the reins of an already-saddled horse.

"We both found it," George agreed. "We should both go."

"And we still need to find a good place for the mill," Ahmed added. The boy looked unusually stubborn, his jaw out and his brow drawn. His projects were the only things that could make him set aside his normal shyness. "We can't forget about it."

"I wasn't going to," Amaya said mildly. She stifled a sigh.

"Let him come!" Drake, former leader of Esteben's Men, spoke up. He inclined his head at Ahmed as he continued. "He's already done the trip once, after all, right?"

Amaya sighed. There was no good argument against it, really.

"I've already packed my own food," Ahmed said. "I won't be a problem."

"If anything were to happen to you, Vasha would kill me," Amaya muttered. The boy only lifted his chin higher; he knew he'd won.

"Fine, fine," Amaya said. "But that's it! No one else has any reason to come. We need as many as possible clearing new fields while the weather holds."

Ahmed had done her a favor—the crowd seemed to take this as a final pronouncement and started to disperse. She still heard a good bit of grumbling, but in a minute or two, the square was mostly clear.

Mostly clear except for her ersatz diplomatic envoy, now ten, and their horses.

"I really hope this isn't too many," Amaya muttered, mostly to herself.

"This is barely a hunting party!" Drake informed her, his tone far too cheerful. He had only recently been taken off the far ranger rotation and seemed eager to prove his use to the village. "We'll be fine."

Amaya arched an eyebrow at that. Granted, out of their armor and unarmed, the former raiders were much less intimidating. Some of them had found themselves quickly accepted amongst the Ostons. But even so, they still had a certain way about them, an air of unquestioned authority, a tilt to the head and a heavy tread, that set them apart from the long-time Ostons. Drake, eager as he was to please, still spoke and often acted like his words would be met with unquestioning obedience. Others of the newcomers carried themselves with a certain undefinable superiority—Amaya had thought many times that winter that even wearing the same clothes and bent to the same tasks, it was easy to pick the raiders out from the villagers.

It made her uneasy, and she knew it was unfair of her. The newcomers had stuck to their word and honored the election results. Both of them—though the election held upon Vasha's retirement had been little more than a formality. Amaya had been elected Headwoman nearly unanimously. It was incumbent upon her to act like the leader of a united people.

"We'd better get going if we want to make good time," Devra said. She hiked a foot up into a stirrup and swung herself quickly and easily into the saddle of a tall bay mare. Deetz, her constant shadow, did the same.

"Right," Amaya said. "Well, George, since you know where we're going, why don't you take the lead?"

George nodded and turned, quietly lacing his hands together to boost Ahmed onto the back of his horse. The boy flushed but accepted the help, steadying himself on George's broad shoulder as he flopped into the saddle.

Amaya did her best to imitate the more experienced riders, grabbing the saddle's horn and stepping up on the stirrup. It didn't feel anywhere near as elegant as Devra made it look, but it worked. She reached up to adjust her hijab as she waited for the rest of the party to mount. When everyone was up and looked settled, she gave George a nod.

"We'll ride hard until we get beyond the patrols," George said, pitching his voice to carry. "Anyone has any problems, or notices a problem with their horse, speak up. Better to lose a day than a horse. Follow close, especially once we leave the fields. Anyone need a piss?"

There was a rumble of laughter and a general shaking of heads. With a firm nod, George turned his mount and kicked his heels, setting a steady canter. One by one, the other members of the party fell in behind. When it came to her turn, Amaya found she barely had to touch her feet to her mount's side before it took off, eager to fall in line with the rest.

There was a lesson in that, somewhere. Something about trusting the wisdom of the crowd and following the will of the majority even if you didn't know where they headed—even if they didn't know. Amaya decided she would ponder it as she hunched down and held on to the horse's mane for dear life.

———

Jacob knocked quietly on the door and pushed his way in without waiting for a response. The plate he carried was easier to balance than last night's dinner had been—Old Ben had given him one with a slight dent on one side meant to serve as a grip as it was carried around the Shelter. The room was almost exactly as he'd left it the previous night— small and crowded with boxes of stored vegetables and grain, with a worn, haphazard construction up against the far wall that served as a bed if you squinted at it long enough. If this was really where Vasha slept, the old woman hadn't exactly been claiming any privileges for her station. Pa lay in the same spot he'd eased himself into last night before Jacob had left.

"Pa? Got your breakfast. Toast and honey. It's real nice."

There was no response from the figure on the bed.

"Pa?" Jacob called again. He started to shut the door behind him, then reconsidered and left it open when he realized how dark the room was. He took the few strides to the bed and set the plate down on a small, boxy side table.

"Your lantern's gone out, Pa. Let me get you some light."

But as he reached for the lantern, a thin hand snaked out from the bed and grabbed him by the wrist.

"What's happening out there?" Jon Newsome hissed. His eyes gleamed up at his son. "What am I hearing about another village?"

"You're hearing that?" Jacob's eyes widened, and he found himself reconsidering his assumptions about how his father had spent the night.

"Talk to me, boy."

"Uh . . ." Jacob cast a glance toward the open door and lowered his voice. "George and the kid found another village, 'bout a day and a half away by horse. They said it looked new, and smaller than Osto. A group left this morning to go . . . talk to them, I guess."

"That's it? We don't know anything else?"

Jacob shook his head. "It's on a river. I think they were looking for the river, not the village."

"Obviously," Jon snapped. He released his son's wrist and pulled himself upright in bed. One bony hand plucked at the sheets as he thought. "This might be something. A chance for us. If we can work it right, we can use this."

"Pa . . ." Jacob shook his head. "We got enough to worry about with the house, right?"

"Fah! Forget about the house. It's a ruin, anyway. What we need is to get to that new village. Set ourselves up there. It's a golden opportunity."

Jacob blinked. "What makes you think they'll take us, Pa? Osto barely wants us as it is."

"I didn't say I'd give them a choice." Pa's eyes were narrow, but a glint of something, a spark rekindled, burned in the depths of the blue. "Who went to talk to the new village?"

"Uh . . ." He'd only glanced at the party as the crowd dispersed around it. "Amaya and Drake and George and Ahmed and Deetz and . . . I don't know all the newcomers. And . . ."

"And?"

"And . . . and Ma."

"Traitor!" Jon spat. "I never should have let her out of the house."

"She's . . ." Jacob started, but somehow, he knew Pa wouldn't hear what he had to say. *She's happy, Pa. You didn't let her, she left.*

"Did you say both Amaya and Drake are gone? For at least three days?"

"Yeah . . . I guess. Maybe more, if they stay at the other place."

"And the old bitch is staying away while I'm here. This is . . . this is better than I could have hoped." Jon grinned, and it was somehow worse than his sour frown. "Listen, son. Listen close. I need you to go out to the raiders' buildings for me. I need you to deliver a message. Y'got anything to write with?"

"Uh, no, but I can go get—"

"No! Don't do anything different than normal. Don't draw any attention. We need to be careful. When you come back with lunch, bring paper and ink. I need time to think, anyway."

"All right, but you got to eat breakfast, Pa," Jacob said. He stood. "And I'm gonna refill the lamp."

"Fuck the lamp!" Jon snarled, but there didn't seem to be any real venom behind it. "Go. Come back at lunch. We'll talk then."

"All right, Pa," Jacob said. He hesitated. "It's . . . good to see you up."

The only reply he got was a snort of derision. Jacob hesitated, but when he saw his father reach for the plate of toast, he nodded to himself and stepped back.

"See you later, Pa."

His father waved him away and took his first bite of the toast and honey.

DAY 4

They had broken camp at sunrise and started the second day of the ride in the murky morning light. Amaya found herself very glad George was there—the man seemed to have an uncanny wayfinding ability and a near-perfect memory for the hazards they'd previously encountered and could thus now avoid. It meant she could let someone else lead, for once, and spend her time worrying about how to approach the strangers in the new village.

Knowing they had built at least a few permanent structures was encouraging. That meant they intended to put down roots, weren't planning on moving closer, and weren't afraid of hard work. The children were another encouraging sign—family life made one crave peace and prosperity. Roving bands of raiders didn't tend to have children with them.

Amaya had spent most of her early life in a mixed traveling group that called itself a cafila. They had roamed the grasslands to the south, staying at one camp for a few months, foraging for whatever was in season, and then moving north as the weather warmed, or south as it cooled. It had seemed the best possible way to survive at the time—they never exhausted the food supply around them, they avoided the worst of the weather's rage, and they were never in any one place long enough for word to get around and dangerous hordes to come looking for easy looting.

In a way, the cafila had been much like Osto. Everyone did whatever they could to help the group, and every adult watched over all the children. They'd been led by a council of the oldest members of each family, rather than a single leader; Amaya was coming to appreciate that more now. No single leader meant no one person took the blame for wrong decisions or lapses of judgment.

Perhaps this new village was like her cafila and had decided the time had come to settle in a relatively safe place. Perhaps—she let herself dare to hope for a brief moment—it might even include some other survivors of her old band. It had been a long time since the fire had destroyed and scattered them, but she was certain she'd recognize any of them.

"Stop here!" George called. He hardly needed to say it—when he halted his mount, the other horses all did the same, as they had been trained to do. George reined around to face the rest of them and came as close as he could to Amaya's side.

"Any further, and they'll be able to see us through the trees," he said. He pointed forward, and Amaya could see the thinning of the trees, indicating the end of the forest. "About half a klick that way."

"Right . . ." Amaya bit her lip. She hadn't devised any plan during the ride—foolish nostalgia had run away with her thoughts. "We're Ostons. We mean no harm. We'll approach on foot—"

A protest cry rose from one of the newcomers. "We already carry no weapons. They'll be able to see that," one of them said. "We shouldn't be taking any more risks."

Amaya frowned. She didn't know this one's name—he hadn't done much to distinguish himself since arrival—but Drake seemed to trust him. "All right, some of us will approach on foot," she amended. "Me, Drake, George, and Devra. The rest can come behind on the horses. But I want them to see us willing to meet them on the ground."

"Sounds good to me," Devra said flatly.

Deetz gave a grunt, and she shot him a grin. "You can sweep me off my feet if there's trouble."

Amaya was glad for the quick agreement; it stifled further protest. With a nod, she swung down from the saddle and almost collapsed as her legs turned to jelly. She managed not to cry out even as she clung to the tack. Sensation slowly pinned and needled back into her limbs.

Drake, George, and Devra had a much easier time of it, but they all had more experience riding than she did. Mercifully, none of them said anything as she held her breath, waiting for the feeling to pass. When it did, she handed the reins of her horse to one of the newcomers. She nodded at her three fellow emissaries, and they made their way through the trees at a slow, careful pace, the string of riders trailing behind. Her legs ached worse than anything she'd felt in years. Maybe the short walk would help, but she didn't hold out much hope for it.

The forest floor turned rocky, and the soil changed, the trees going thin and scraggly. The underbrush grew thicker as the canopy thinned, and then suddenly, they weren't in a forest but a broad, sloping patch of grass and scrub. George paused just under the last tree and scanned ahead, but Amaya caught her breath an instant before he pointed.

There it was, just as described—a cluster of wooden structures and tents occupying a stretch of the grassland halfway between the forest and a broad, slow-moving river. It was every bit as eclectic as she'd been led to believe—large tents, wagons, a few small, round huts. Everywhere hung banners, flags, and canopies dyed in surprisingly deep, bright colors. A few people moved about the buildings, though not nearly as many as she'd have expected at this time of day. And— there—five children, playing in the mud flats by the river and overseen by a single adult figure.

Every bit as peaceful as she'd hoped. Amaya felt her heart lighten. A smile played on her lips as she watched the smallest child, barely old enough to walk, fall head-on into the mud. Two of the others helped the little one up, but a fourth laughed so boldly they could almost hear it from their position across the plain. The adult figure stirred, moving over to inspect the filthy child, but in a calm, unhurried way that seemed to indicate no real alarm.

"Well," she said, half to herself and half to the rest of the party. "Come on, then."

It wasn't long after they left the trees that the village seemed to notice them. The distant sound of raised voices reached them, though no words could be made out just yet. More people appeared from wagons and tents, inevitably turning and peering in their direction for a moment or two before hurrying off to some preordained task. As Amaya made her way through the tall grasses, she noted the efficiency and coordination with which they moved, as well as the calmness of their actions. They were either very naive or very, very confident.

By the time she'd reached the edge of the cleared land around the settlement, a small party had assembled to greet them. No children in this delegation but adults of all ages, including one man who looked nearly as old as Vasha. All different skin colors but similar builds—lean and muscular, healthy, well fed. One young woman held a tall pole with a limp banner on it, impossible to read on the windless day, but dyed bright purple and gold. Other than that, they were unarmed. Amaya glanced to her side, trying to read her own party members. Drake and George looked calm, faces kept carefully blank. Devra was aglow with undisguised curiosity, her eyes darting from the welcome party to all points of the small town. Amaya chose to take that as a good sign— Devra was a brilliant hunter and tracker but generally not so fond of people.

Turning back, Amaya summoned a smile and took a deep breath, pitching her voice to carry across the short distance between the two groups.

"Peace be upon you, friends! We come from Osto, your neighbors to the south. We hope to . . ."

"To figure out if you need to worry about us?" The speaker was a tall man in his late thirties, his long dark hair tied back from dark eyes and bronzed skin. "I admit, we've been wondering the same."

"Have you?" Devra asked, and Amaya was glad for it as she processed his words. Apparently, the new village had known about Osto far longer than Osto had known about them.

"We've been meaning to introduce ourselves," the man, apparently the appointed speaker, replied. "But there hasn't been a quiet moment."

"Isn't that always the way?" Devra said, her sarcasm unmistakable.

Amaya gave a soft cough at that. "We're . . . always happy to welcome newcomers in Osto," she said. "What can we call you?"

This seemed to give the man pause. He glanced at his companions, who variously nodded or shrugged at him. Turning back, he gave her a nod himself. "I'm Dan Tallgrass. And this . . ." He waved behind him. "This is the Folklife Department of the University of Washington at New Tacoma."

There was a moment of silence like they were waiting for some particular response.

"Washington?" Amaya asked.

At the same time, Devra said, "Folklife?"

A laugh went up from the other party, and Dan Tallgrass gave a rueful chuckle. "Fair enough. You can call us the Folk, or Folkies. We've named this place New Tacoma. Have you had lunch? We just started roasting some salmon when you all showed up, and if we don't get back to it, they'll burn. We can throw a few more on for you folks."

It was as good an offer as anyone could expect. They didn't get fish often in Osto—the small creeks near them rarely had more than minnows. Amaya turned to her party, expectant. A moment passed as she waited for someone to voice an opinion. Then, with a jolt, she realized they were waiting for her to lead.

"All right," she said, trying to sound more confident than she felt. "Let's go. Dismount, all."

"You can tie your horses up by the river," Dan added. "They can graze and drink there. Grace will show you."

A willowy young woman with night-dark skin and sharp cheekbones took a step forward. She smiled at them all. "Follow me, please. We'll meet back at the fire circle."

Without waiting for a response, Grace started to lead away from the main village. After harried discussions, half the Ostons followed. Ahmed silently handed the reins of his horse to Deetz and ran up behind George, standing in his shadow as though hiding. Amaya nodded tacit permission at him and gave silent thanks that no one felt the need to argue for once.

That left her with Devra, Drake, George, Ahmed, and the party of . . . Folk?

"It's still a bit cold in the mornings, yeah?" Dan Tallgrass was saying. "We've taken to keeping a fire going all the time. Lower in the day, of course, but it's a real lifesaver at night. How do you stay warm in Osto?"

"Fire," Amaya answered. She stepped closer to him, crossing from the tall grass of the plain into the cropped fields surrounding the town. "Most of us live in a large building where we keep the kitchen fires going at all times."

"Stoves have chimneys that cross the ceiling," George added. "Uses residual heat to keep the place warm."

"Oh . . . yes." Amaya blinked. She hadn't actually known that, and she'd lived in Osto a lot longer than George had. She'd never really thought about how the heat worked, just given silent thanks that it always did.

"And textiles?" Dan asked. "What do you use for blankets? Your clothes look a lot more sophisticated than some places we've seen. How many people do you have?"

"Uh . . ." Amaya frowned. Why was he so curious? Why did he want to know? Could she have misjudged? They didn't have another two hundred people hiding in the trees waiting to attack, did they?

"Everyone in Osto does a little spinning or weaving." Devra had jumped into the silence when Amaya didn't answer. "Especially the kids, when they're too young for other work."

"Brilliant," Dan Tallgrass said, beaming. The smile looked genuine; it lit up his entire face. "Get everyone involved in manufacturing; that's how you do it. You'd be shocked how many places haven't figured that out yet."

"Oh?" Amaya said, raising her eyebrows. She wasn't exactly interested in his opinion of Osto's work balance, but the mention of other towns was more intriguing. "Do tell."

"Oh! Well . . ." he glanced toward the mounted contingent, still making their way to the riverbank. "Why don't we wait until everyone's together to talk? In the meantime, can we show you around and offer you some snacks? The fish will take a while, but we always have some staples on hand."

Amaya filed away the dodge as something to be carefully considered later and found a smile for the offer. "We would be honored, thank you."

"Come on, then. Everyone's been very patient, but I know they're eager to meet you."

The fire circle was an unassuming name for what turned out to be the focal point of the village. A large cleared area in the middle of the gathered wagons and tents, almost a plaza, surrounded a carefully constructed low stone circle filled with ash and embers nearly ten feet across. Metal racks lined the entire inside wall, though the only active fire glowed underneath several grills loaded with bright silver salmon, roasting whole. The pit was surrounded by several layers of split-log benches. Amaya felt her heart lift as she realized she was looking at a communal kitchen every bit as vital as the one in the Shelter.

A young man who had been tending the fires stood as they approached. "Dan?"

Dan nodded at him. "These fine visitors are going to be joining us for lunch, Pat. Ten in total."

"Ten?" Pat frowned at the fire, seeming to do a quick mental calculation. "That'll be two more, then. We should still have enough in the weir. I'll go get them."

"Thanks, man. And can you tell Nana we could use some of her preserves and bread?"

"Will do." Pat gave one of the roasting fish a slight poke with a stick. Whatever that told him seemed satisfactory, as he then turned and left the circle, heading not for the river but for one of the colorful wagons set back in the village.

"Hope you all like fish," Dan Tallgrass said. He waved them to seats on the first row of benches even as he moved closer to the firepit. "It's pretty much all we've got at the moment. But we have plans to change that."

"Plans?" Amaya asked, trying to sound as neutral as possible. She sat on the indicated bench, and Devra and Drake sat to her left. George, for some reason, seemed to have taken an interest in one of the tall strings of banners that flew around the circle, and wandered quietly away from the group. Ahmed followed George, listening closely to whatever the man was muttering.

"Well, maybe you could even help us out with that," Dan said. "We've heard of Osto, of course. Well, not by name. But rumor spreads, you know. We keep hearing tales of a big village that's welcome to all. You must have a real farm going, right? Livestock and all? I mean, it's been ages since we saw anyone else with domesticated horses."

It was almost disorienting to realize how much this stranger already knew about them when she knew so little about him and his people. Amaya blinked, trying to place it all. He was right, of course—the rumors had drawn her and Umair north after the cafila had collapsed, just as they had brought Drake and his men east.

"The horses are new," she said, opting for a relatively safe answer. "But we grow what we can, yes."

"Fascinating," Dan said. He picked up Pat's stick and scraped at the dirt, sending small puffs of ash and dust into the air. "And it's doing okay? Not sickly or . . .?"

"Osto's fields have been worked for decades," Devra said. "It took a while, but we've crops that grow true."

"We would love to hear how you did that," Dan said. "Or to trade even, since I imagine we'll need the support while we figure out—"

A voice from behind them interrupted. "I'm told we have guests, and I'm told it by young Pat Crannigan?"

Amaya turned to see an older woman making her way towards the group. Short and broad, heaving along a large, elaborately woven basket, she hurried toward them with an ease that belied the age implied by her thick white hair.

"'Ey, Nana, I sent him specially for you," Dan called, a smile breaking across his face.

"You sent him for my jam, you mean. Didn't think to come yourself? Or bring our guests round to visit?"

"It's not quite . . ." Dan paused, then seemed to give the argument up for lost. "Well, it's good you're here now, Nana. I can introduce you."

"I can introduce myself, boyo," the woman said.

Amaya found herself grinning. Somehow, the interplay put her more at ease than anything else she had seen so far.

The woman (Nana?) picked her way among the benches until she was facing them. Up close, the lines of her weathered face were deep but good-natured. She had dark skin and a halo of tight white curls and wore a brightly striped shawl over a simple dress. Amaya found herself staring at the vivid blue of the dress—almost a perfect summer sky at noon, unlike any color she'd ever seen on fabric.

"Hello, guests. I'm Fantra, senior herbalist and botanist. Friends call me Nana, but we're not there yet. I was told you'd be hungry?"

"Er, well," Amaya started.

"Are you hungry or not?" Fantra asked. She set her basket on a bench and started digging around in it.

"It is lunch time," Amaya managed. Truth be told, her stomach was in too many knots to really consider eating, but she wasn't going to turn down an offer of food for the whole party.

"What's a botanist?" Devra asked.

"Means I'm good at growing plants," Fantra answered. She set out a wrapped bundle and carefully unwrapped it to reveal a stack of flatbreads. They were thinner than what Osto usually produced and flecked with seeds of some kind. "Know a lot about it when I'm in the right place."

"And this is the right place?" Amaya asked, curious.

"Could be," Fantra grunted. She was still setting things out from her basket—another bundle of flatbreads, some wooden knives, and then, casually as you please, two small, glistening jars that could only have been made of glass.

Behind her, Amaya heard Ahmed catch his breath. He must have been lured back to the group by the promise of food.

"That's one's apple and that one's persimmon," Fantra was saying, pointing at each jar in turn. "We've got saplings of both we're hoping to plant soon."

"And . . . glass?" Ahmed, apparently finished with his examination of the banners, pushed between Devra and Amaya to get a closer look at the jars. He eagerly reached for one, hesitated, and then let his curiosity get the better of him and grabbed up the persimmon jar.

"That's Gemma's work. You'd have to talk to her," Fantra said. She gave Ahmed a narrow look. "The *jam* is mine."

The boy held the jar up to the sun, which shone through the glass and the dark orange preserves within. The material was clear and colorless, with hundreds of tiny bubbles that seemed to concentrate near the bottom of the vessel. A rim of broken red wax lined the lip of the jar where the lid sat.

"This is new glass," Ahmed breathed. "You *made* it."

Amaya sat up a little straighter as the implications of Ahmed's words suddenly became clear. Since their arrival, they'd seen masses of fabric used almost negligently, dye colors she'd never imagined, and now glass —often found shattered or broken on scavenging trips, treasured the rare times a vessel or pane was discovered whole. She'd never even heard of anyone who still knew how to make it.

"As I said, you'd have to ask Gemma," Fantra said, holding out a piece of flatbread for the boy. "Are you hungry or not?"

Ahmed took the bread with an expression that could only be called a pout and set to spreading it with preserves. He opened the jar with reverence and seemed loath to replace it on the bench when he was done. Amaya took a piece of bread to be polite, and one by one, Devra, Drake, and finally George claimed some as well. The bread was thin and crisp, uneven on top, and packed with tangy, brittle seeds. The apple jam was a smooth and easy spread that softened the sharpness of the seeds and blunted the jagged bits of the bread, turning an unpleasant staple into an easy snack. Fantra watched as they ate, seeming to take deep satisfaction in the surprised, pleased reactions each gave as they tried the jam. She didn't even object when Ahmed grabbed a jar again, showing it to George and whispering questions.

As they ate, the rest of the party returned from the riverbank. They'd picked up more villagers during their diversion and seemed to have several conversations going at once. As they joined, the Ostons took seats on the first and second row of benches, the Folkies surrounded them, and a pleasant hum of conversation rose as everyone ate and exchanged names and sized each other up.

Soon enough, Pat returned with a few more salmon and added them to the grills, then declared the previous set done and ready to serve. This caused a flurry of activity as plates and utensils were produced, and more Folkies emerged from tents and huts to join them for lunch. Before long, the entire fire circle was full of people and crowded with conversation. The Ostons found themselves the focus of a good many curious looks even as they were plied with food and drink.

In the midst of the friendly chaos, Amaya turned back to Dan. "Maybe you can start by telling us exactly what a Folklife Department is," she said.

Dan smiled back at her. "It's a long story," he replied. "But first off, do you know what a university is?"

Only in the vaguest of terms. Amaya pursed her lips. "Not really."

Dan sighed. "So much of the old world is slipping away. Most don't even know what we've lost."

"Like you were there," Fantra said, rolling her eyes. "Don't be rude, Dan. Just answer the question."

Dan grinned at that. "Yes, Nana." He turned back to Amaya. "Back in the day, in the old world, universities were places where people went to learn. They were like small towns dedicated only to education. People could go there and study things that interested them so they could work."

Amaya wasn't sure she understood. "What did they study?"

Dan sighed. "Lots of things. The old world was bigger . . . or at least, it had more in it. Each university had departments that studied different subjects. And my people, we're from the Folklife Department. My grandparents studied indigenous art and storytelling, and how people passed their histories down the generations. Fantra's father studied medical folkways. Gemma, " he waved at someone across the fire circle, but it wasn't clear who, "her grandparents actually studied textiles and weaving, but she chose to apprentice to Sam and Clyde to study glassblowing and metalworking."

"We have weavers," Amaya said, catching the one familiar term in the flow of information.

Dan beamed. "So do we! Textiles are so under-appreciated. They really can tell the story of a culture, right?"

Amaya blinked. This had the feeling of an old and much-loved argument. "So . . . you're part of one of these universities, then?"

"Ah . . ." Dan waved a hand. "Sort of. We were. We don't know if the University of Washington still exists. Our parents and grandparents, kind of . . . you know . . . When things started getting bad, they decided to leave the city. They gathered everything they thought they might need and left to find a safe place to live."

"And they never stopped moving," Amaya finished. "They never found that place." That much, she understood.

"Until now! Hopefully." Dan's smile this time looked shy. "If you'll have us, anyway. This place is perfect for us for a lot of reasons. We'd like to stay here."

Amaya found herself fighting against an innate urge to be immediately accommodating. "That's certainly what we're here to discuss," she managed.

"Great!" Dan grinned. "Maybe after lunch, I can take you folks around and show you just how much you'd like to have us as neighbors."

"That . . . that would be good," Amaya managed. She stared down at what remained of her fish. Half left. In half a fish, she'd have to start deciding what the future might look like.

She had never felt less prepared.

———

The furnace was a hunched, roaring dragon of a thing, complete with a glowing hot core and scales etched onto its metal carapace. It sat within a framework of thick metal bars that secured it to a platform that must have once had wheels. Gemma, a tall, pale woman with short-cropped white hair, gently leaned back from the glowing maw and drew a long metal rod from it, topped with what looked like a ball of pure, glowing light.

Ahmed had never seen anything more beautiful. "And it's been in constant use since you left? It hasn't broken or needed anything to be replaced or . . . or anything?"

"Well, a few less important things have broken," Gemma said. "It's been easy enough to keep up. It's basically a giant oven made of concrete." She turned the rod gently in her hands as she spoke, her eyes locked on the glowing orb.

"You can repair it?" George asked, a bass rumble behind Ahmed. "Can you make new pieces?"

"We actually have two! The big one hasn't been fully assembled since we left the university." Gemma twirled the stick, watching it closely as though seeking any imperfections. "We use it for reference when pieces break."

"So, you know how to build it all?" George said.

"You're asking if we can make one for your Osto, yeah?" Gemma countered, raising her eyebrows.

Ahmed flushed, but he was glad when George pressed the question. "Can you?"

"That's . . . complicated," Gemma replied. She set the glowing end of the stick on a large, flat work counter and started rolling it slowly and steadily across the surface. The cooling effect was near instant and obvious—the bright white glow turned a dull, throbbing red. "We've got the skills to remake most of it. We could probably reproduce almost all the parts between the smith and the ceramicist. But . . ."

"Almost?" Ahmed felt his heart sink.

"The inside would be the problem. The liner is made of a blend of clay and metal that we don't have the recipe for. Whatever it is, it's real, real strong. It doesn't melt."

"Maybe . . . maybe we could try," Ahmed suggested. "We could figure it out." He glanced back at George, who nodded at the suggestion.

"Maybe! That's actually one of the reasons we're here."

Ahmed's eyes widened, and he turned back to Gemma. "It is?"

"Well, sort of." Gemma slowed the roll of the rod and raised it carefully. "Illinois was supposed to have had some of the best glass sand in the world, once upon a time. We wanted to see if it's still here."

"Is it?"

"It's sure better than anything else I've seen," Gemma said. During their entire conversation, she never once took her eyes off the glowing orb at the end of the stick.

Ahmed couldn't tear his eyes away, either. He noted how quickly the mass of light responded to motion; how, if ever she stopped or slowed the turning, the ball started to deform almost instantly in a slow slump.

"Is it glass now? You don't have to do anything else to it?"

"It will be when it cools off," Gemma said. She laid the rod down in a notch on the far edge of her workbench and quickly glanced up at the boy. "Watch this."

Without warning, she stood back, set her lips to the end of the stick, and blew. The molten glass stretched in response, going thin and clear and brittle. Ahmed stifled a gasp, which was apparently exactly the reaction she'd been looking for. She gave them both a wicked grin.

"Got to get the shape in there somehow! Fantra's been after me to make her some bigger jars."

Ahmed started to inch closer, only to be stopped by a heavy hand on his shoulder. He glanced up at George, hurt that he'd hold him back, but his friend gave him a rueful smile.

"Give the woman her room, kid; you don't know what she might need that space for."

"Some techniques do involve a lot of swinging," Gemma agreed cheerfully. "Not anything I'm doing today, though."

"Swinging? Why?" Ahmed asked, perfectly willing to be distracted.

"Lengthens it out. Good for making tall vases or starting tubes. That or spinning's how you get flat glass," Gemma replied. She chose a tool from a tray near the work surface, hiked her grip up the rod, and started scoring into the jar. "Things like mirrors, window panes, like that. If we can find the right sand, I want to try lenses someday."

"Lenses!" Ahmed barely managed to resist the power of temptation —he did *not* push his glasses up his nose. "Like for glasses?"

"I assume yours were scavenged?" Gemma glanced up from her work just long enough to see Ahmed nod. "You're a lucky kid, then. Lots of people could use glasses like that, but finding a surviving pair that fits your eyes is rare. Could use some myself, really. Imagine if we could rediscover how to make them."

"You could make magnifiers," George offered. "Even for people who don't need glasses."

"And more than that," Gemma's voice went soft and dreamy. "They used lenses for all kinds of things, once. Magnifiers you could point at the stars and see other worlds in the sky."

"Baba said my dad had one, once," Ahmed offered. He almost didn't want to intrude. "He called it a telescope."

"'Tele' for distance, 'scope' for sight," Gemma agreed. She shook her head, as though reminding herself of the task at hand. "Someday. We'll get there."

So many of the old technologies he'd read about relied on glass parts, lenses, bottles, or screens. Ahmed's head swam with the possibilities— everything from telescopes and magnifiers to windows and doors. He could make or repair his own glasses or give them to everyone in Osto. Jars and bottles would open up new possibilities for food preservation over the winter. They could replace all the missing lantern panes or make new shades to protect candles from drafts. With the ability to make glass, he could bring light and warmth and plenty to the cold, dark, hungry winters of Osto.

Ahmed glanced back, wondering if George was as excited as he was by the possibilities, only to find the big man staring, transfixed, not at the glowing glass or the furnace, but at Gemma herself.

Well. That was beside the point.

———

Devra, Deetz, and several of the newcomers obediently followed their appointed tour guide. It had been an eye-opening introduction to the necessities of life as a recently nomadic people, at least. Until now, the Folk had kept no livestock, raised no crops, and kept only those items they could fit on their motley collection of wagons and pack animals. They'd already encountered at least three people full of grand plans to build and expand now that they were "settled."

Devra had some thoughts about that. Nothing she was willing to share just yet, but judging by Deetz's skeptical grunts and the quiet looks of alarm the other newcomers exchanged when they thought no one was looking, she wasn't the only one.

They were currently looking at the partially cleared field beyond the main bulk of the village. Their guide pointed at an area that had been noticeably plowed.

"Nana's been collecting seeds and cuttings from everywhere we've been," he said. Pat was a boy in his older teens with a wide face and bright eyes. He seemed to have endless enthusiasm for nearly everything and absolutely no sense that he might ever need to hold anything back from the visitors.

"We're hoping to plant them as soon as we get the field ready and maybe get some fruit next year or the year after."

"Might take longer than that," Devra said. "I understand some plants take five or ten years to fruit."

There was a barely perceptible pause. "We'll find out! A lot of these are wild fruits that we don't know much about! Have you ever had gooseberry jam?"

"Can't say as I have," Devra replied.

"Maybe soon! Oh! If you come this way, I can show you the fish weirs."

Devra stifled a sigh. The tour had crisscrossed the village so much already that she was prone to suspect that the boy had been told to keep them busy and distracted, even though she'd been there when Dan Tallgrass had singled out the kid and asked him to take them around. Nonetheless, if Amaya wanted them to play nice with the strangers, they'd play nice. She turned and followed Pat as he angled upriver, just north of the village itself.

The weirs, when they reached them, were the most impressive structures they'd seen yet. Across a broad, shallow stretch of the river, a series of sturdy carved stakes had been driven into the riverbed, far apart enough to let water and small fish through but close enough to force larger fish to turn and follow the makeshift wall until they reached the inlet of a closed circular area. Three of these constructs stretched across the river at various points, and two of the closed areas visibly teemed with the silvery fish they'd had for lunch. Devra raised her eyebrows, appreciating the simple ingenuity and the many hours of physical labor that had gone into creating such a system.

"We're saving up any large stones we find clearing the fields," Pat was saying. "So eventually, we can replace the wood and make it permanent. We didn't get much when it was cold, but it's been really picking up since the weather got warmer, and soon, we'll start drying and preserving them for next winter."

"What'll you do when the river floods?" asked one of the newcomers, a tall, blond man Devra had only recently learned was called Sorsch.

"Floods?" Pat asked, quizzical as though the question had never occurred to him. "I guess we'll—hey! Hey! Daisy!"

Pat's easily catchable attention had been snagged by the sudden appearance of a small, furry creature on the riverbank. With large, pointed ears and a short, upheld tail, it picked its way down to the water with caution, suggesting the inexperience of the very young. Even so, it paid no attention whatsoever to Pat's call, and the boy took off running with not a single glance backward.

"No! Bad kitten! Stop!"

Devra found herself smiling for the first time since the tour had started. A touch at her shoulder made her glance back at Deetz, grinning like the fool he was.

"Can we?" he asked.

"We're supposed to follow our guide, right?" Devra replied, and they jogged after the boy, leaving Sorsch and the other newcomers milling in confusion.

The small creature had picked its way down the riverbank easily enough, but it seemed to be hesitating now that it had reached the water itself. This gave Pat enough time to make his own, less careful way down the bank. The kitten finally looked up at him as he approached, glanced back at the rushing water behind it, and then made a dash away from it and off to Pat's left. The boy dodged to the side, blocking its exit, and the kitten broke into a run. Pat dived, his arms outstretched, and managed to get one hand around its small body even as he fell face-first into the mud. The creature let out a thin yowl that could have woken the dead had it been any louder, but Pat had a firm grip on it even as he sat up, beaming in triumph.

"Got you! Let's get you home, you clever thing."

Up close, the "clever thing" had wide, round eyes, tiny whiskers, and paws that seemed far too large for its pudgy little body. It flailed at the fingers that held it but had no success freeing itself.

"What . . . what *is* that?" Devra asked. It had all the hallmarks of a bobcat, but she'd never seen one so small. Or so clumsy.

"Daisy? She's a kitten. A baby cat." Pat gave her a quizzical look.

"A bobcat? A . . . a mountain cat?"

"No, just . . . just a cat." Pat frowned. "Do you not have cats?"

"Seen 'em, but never kept one," Deetz replied. He stepped forward and bent down until he was at eye level with the tiny thing.

"Oh, you have to come see, then! Quickfoot had six kittens, and they're all doing really well. It's just Daisy here that keeps escaping."

"Take us," Devra gasped. "Right now."

Daisy yowled a protest, but no one listened to her.

———

Sarah Newsome had not been able to contain her curiosity. After lunch, she followed Fantra to a large, colorful wagon amongst the tents and huts. It was her first chance to get a good look at one, and up close, the bright colors were chipped enough to suggest years of wear, exposure to the elements, and careful, loving upkeep. The back half of the wagon was entirely enclosed in wood, while the front half had a canvas covering that could be removed and repurposed as a tarp or awning. The whole construction was sunk far enough into the soft mud of the riverbank that moving it again would be a formidable undertaking.

"If you don't mind . . ." Sarah began, hesitating.

Fantra turned, keeping both hands on the basket. "Of course not, dear. Why would I mind?"

"Oh, I just . . ." Sarah shook her head, trying to deny the instant compulsion to apologize. "You mentioned you have saplings? And other samples? I'd love to see them."

A wide smile broke across the old woman's wrinkled face. "Of course, of course! Come in!"

Sarah hesitated, watching the woman balance her basket, heft it up into the wagon, and then climb up after it. A rickety stair led up into the wagon itself, the interior of which was dark enough compared to the midday sun that she could see nothing within. After a moment, she took a breath, squared her shoulders, and followed.

Once her eyes adjusted, Sarah caught her breath in delight. The inside of the wagon was a fairytale of plant lore. Nearly every surface, save a single work counter at the back, was covered in dried or drying flowers, leaves, and small bundles of twigs. One wall was lined entirely with tiny drawers labeled in scrawled handwriting, while the other hosted shallow shelves filled with jewel-bright glass jars. Everywhere, the scent of herbs known and unknown, of fresh-cut grass, of old, powdery dried flowers combined and overlapped into a heady, overpowering sensory assault.

It could not have been more different from her clean and orderly infirmary, yet she knew, somehow, this place served the same function.

"The saplings and live plants are in the front, where they can get some sun," Fantra said. "Though we've started some seedlings already out in the garden. What were you interested in?"

Sarah barely had a moment to collect her thoughts before they were interrupted by a soft knock outside the wagon's wall, and a Folk girl stuck her head inside.

"Hello, Nana." The newcomer smiled. She was a tall girl, brown with sun, and rangy from years of physical labor. Her black hair was long but tied back, and her light linen dress almost glowed in contrast.

"Paisley, dear, it's always good to see your face." Fantra broke into a smile warmer than what she'd offered Sarah.

"'Lo, Nana. It's good to see you, too." Paisley gave Sarah a curious look. "I'm sorry, I didn't realize you'd be busy. I'll come back."

"Nonsense, darling. What is it?"

Paisley bit her lip, still eyeing Sarah, but then seemed to shrug off her presence. "It's not much. I just, uh, need more of that tea. The mugwort?"

"Ah, of course. Do you know how long . . . ?"

Paisley shook her head, then frowned a moment. "I'm . . . a week late, I think? But I don't know when exactly."

Fantra nodded. "A thin mixture should do, then. Let me see what I've got."

The woman made her way into the depths of the wagon, and now Sarah understood the purpose of the many tiny drawers. As Fantra moved, she picked up a small burlap sack and a spoon. She went from one side of the wagon to the other, opening drawers and peering inside, deciding for or against whatever she saw. Finally, she stopped at one and pulled out a sprig of wizened brown leaves, which she carefully crumbled off the stem into the bag. Two other stems from different drawers followed, though Sarah could see no discernible difference between them. As she reached the counter, Fantra gently mixed the leaves within the bag with her fingers and added one more from a bunch hanging near a small window.

"There we go. Make sure it only steeps for two minutes, now, and take no more than one mug a day. One normal mug, you hear, none of those huge things Inger's making."

Paisley smiled as she took the bag. "Thank you, Nana. I will. I'm always careful."

"I know you are," Fantra said, nodding. "But see that anyone you share it with is, too, you hear? I don't want anyone getting sick because they were afraid to face me."

Paisley's eyes bugged out—clearly, she'd been caught for her part in some ruse. "What? Frightened? Of you?"

Fantra snorted. "Is it the Bradley girl? She's been scared of me since she was a tiny thing."

The younger woman hesitated before sighing and nodding. "Becca's only been married three months. She's not ready to be a mother yet. She's scared."

"But not scared enough to come face me." Fantra sniffed. "If she can't get over such a childish fear, she's certainly not ready for children of her own. Maybe she's smarter than I give her credit for. Don't tell her I said that."

"I won't," Paisley said, with a small smile. She looked down at the bag she held, contemplative. Then she nodded again, just once. "I'll make sure she comes herself next time, Nana."

Another snort. "I'll believe it when I see it. You're a good friend, Paisley."

"Thank you, Nana. Have a good day." The woman waved as she turned to leave, then belatedly turned and gave Sarah a quick nod. Then she ducked out, leaving the wagon creaking behind her.

In the silence left behind, Sarah frowned, trying to make sense of the interaction. "Did you just . . . I mean, nothing I know will make pregnancy easier."

"Oh, sweet." The old woman's wrinkled face fell into a smile. "She wasn't looking to make it easier. She was looking to make it stop."

"Make it . . ." Sarah blinked. "You can do that?"

The older woman regarded her with a thoughtful, solemn expression. "Yes. It's not even hard, if you catch it in time."

"And . . ." Sarah felt her breath catch in her chest. "And it's okay? Won't . . . won't Becca's husband be angry?"

Fantra waved this off. "Derek is a sweet boy, but he's no more ready to be a father than Becca is to be a mother. But it's not up to him, is it? Becca gets to decide what happens to her own body. Even if she can't get over herself enough to see me in person."

"That's . . ." A finger of fear ran cold down her back. Sarah shivered. "That sounds . . . right."

"It most certainly is right." Fantra huffed to herself and settled onto a worn stool. Then she peered closely at Sarah's face. Whatever she saw there made her narrow her eyes. "Would you like to know how to mix it?"

Sarah paled.

"Me?"

"You. You're a healer, aren't you? I could see your interest in my work."

Stop a pregnancy? Could she do that? It had never even occurred to her before, but somehow, she knew it was wrong.

Wait

No.

She knew where that thought came from. It wasn't *hers*. That unthinking certainty, that unquestioning obedience—if she examined it, she knew it came from Jon. It was a reaction that had been instilled in her by years of his anger and rage, by his dogged insistence on dominance, his driving need for submission. He had been the one who insisted they keep trying for sons. He had been the one who saw his children as a point of pride, not for their achievements and personhood, but for the sheer number of them upon whom he could enforce his will.

Eric was a fine boy of thirteen now, but he'd been her sixth child and the hardest birth.

She'd feared getting pregnant again for years and employed every trick she could think of to avoid it. When her monthlies had stopped, she'd felt nothing but incredible relief—relief that she'd made it out alive, that Jon's bullheadedness hadn't driven her to an early grave.

Sarah had seen what a pregnancy gone wrong could do to a woman. She'd guided both her sisters and three of her daughters-in-law through difficult pregnancies and births, and the ones she'd failed haunted her to this day. Jon had raged for days at the loss of his third grandson, little Adam, who had been born three months too early, blue and gasping and so, so small. His mother, Johanna, had been ill for her entire pregnancy, and the birth had only confirmed their worst fears. She had never borne another child.

Somehow, Jon was convinced it was Johanna's fault.

Stop a pregnancy? Like it was a choice? The thought gave her a strange sense of giddiness, as though a freedom she'd never dreamed of had just been offered to her—and to all the generations of women who would come after her.

———

Indigo, lilac, aqua—these were words she had only ever heard applied to flowers before. Russet, scarlet, saffron—those were words for sunsets. Emerald and jade, those were trees and leaves. But before her, stretched across the drying racks, were bolts of fabric—fabric dyed every color she could think to name and more she was sure she'd never heard of. Amaya had to work to contain her delight at the sight. She'd never been too interested in the specifics of making clothing, but these made her fingers itch to touch, to work, to design something beautiful and bring it into the world.

"We would, of course, be happy to trade," Dan said. He was

watching her from the door of the drying hut, grinning at her reaction. "Both the finished cloth and the techniques to dye it."

It wasn't the first time he'd mentioned trade. Amaya sighed to herself and forced her thoughts away from the dazzling fabrics. She had a duty. Might as well just be blunt about it. "So, what is it, exactly, that you're asking for?"

Dan stepped further inside. His face was suddenly serious. "We have most of what we need. We gather as we travel and preserve what we can. But we're also used to trading with those we come across to supplement our food supply. The things we can't raise ourselves when we're on the move."

Amaya already knew what was coming. She remembered all too well the stresses of the nomadic lifestyle. "You're looking for vegetables. Fruits. Grains."

Dan nodded. "Exactly. Though really, grains more than anything. Now that we're staying in one place, our animals eat through the pastures faster than the grass can regrow, and we need to find another way to feed them."

She nodded. Osto was facing the same issue with their sudden acquisition of horses. "How many? Or how much?"

He smiled broadly as though he'd thought she would turn him down immediately, and this was already a better reception than he'd expected.

Perhaps she should have.

"We'd be looking for about a quarter ton of grain. Wheat, oats, whatever you have. That would be enough to plant and keep horses and people alive until harvest."

She blinked. "What's a ton?"

"It's . . ." Dan frowned, apparently not expecting a math problem. "Hold on, how do you reckon grain?"

Nightfall in Osto was a matter of closings and windings-down. Workers straggled in from the fields. Rangers returned from their patrols. Friends greeted each other after a long day of separation. Each night in Osto had a feeling of finality, of weary rest after long labor, of a community gathering in the commons to eat and gossip and celebrate the successful end of one more day.

Night in the riverside village had a distinctly different flavor.

Somehow, even though it was less than a quarter the size of Osto, the New Tacoma village center felt fuller and louder than the Shelter ever did, life, noise, and laughter crowding in on all sides. As darkness fell, the Folkies built the fire into a blazing roar, a wild, glowing heart of welcome. People poured in all at once—craftfolk and fieldhands and who knew what else, bringing their contributions to the evening meal and also their questions and friendly, lingering stares.

Amaya's relief grew as each member of the Oston delegation reappeared. While Drake had never left her side, the others had each wandered off with various guides, and she had felt surprisingly alone without the full complement. But now, as the fire roared and the full-throated, cheerful evening closed in, the Ostons closed ranks once again. Amaya gestured them over to one of the few huts of the village, which Dan Tallgrass had offered them the use of for the night. As they filed in and the walls muffled the surrounding chaos, she let herself relax for the first time since they'd left home.

The relief was all too short-lived, however.

"You can't be thinking of agreeing." Drake had been surprisingly restrained all afternoon, but as soon as they were alone, it seemed he could no longer contain himself. "They're offering us nothing!"

"I rather thought their offer was a generous one," Amaya replied, narrowing her eyes. "They don't seem to be holding back much of anything."

"They have glass!" This was Ahmed, his eyes wide with a rare excitement. "A full furnace and everything they need to make more! Gemma said they would share it with us!"

"They've gathered herbs and medicines from all across the land," Sarah added. "And in a few years, they may have fruits and crops we've never seen."

"And we still need access to the river," George's deep rumble made everything he said sound like a final pronouncement. "It would be . . . good to stay friends."

"All good arguments," Amaya replied. She grimaced. "But most of you didn't hear what they were asking for."

Expectant eyes watched her. The noise of the crowd outside seemed to swell.

Amaya sighed. "Food. Grains and seed to start their own fields and a share of our winter stores."

"What winter stores?" Drake prodded. "We both know how skint this winter was. We only made it because we hunted."

"We didn't cut into the seed grain . . . did we?" Sarah rarely concerned herself with the more administrative aspects of the village, but she'd been sharing Amaya's mealtimes long enough to know the concern.

"We didn't," Amaya agreed. "But it was a near thing."

"What about livestock?" Devra, rarely comfortable at such gatherings, had the sort of voice that made all fall quiet to hear when she spoke. "We should have a good few kids and lambs this year, I think. Enough to trade, for sure. And from the amount of fabric we've seen around, they should value the sheep highly."

"Possible," Amaya agreed. "But that won't be the food they're looking for. Did you notice dinner was the same fish we had for lunch?"

"Won't last," Deetz said. "Those fish come through in the early spring, not all year long."

Amaya's eyebrows rose at that. She'd never quite understood what Devra saw in her raider, but if he had more knowledge like that hidden away . . . "We can't let them starve," she said.

"We can't starve ourselves to help them," Drake replied. "What good would their glass or medicine be to us if we all die hungry? We owe them nothing! They came to our territory!"

"This is a good bit farther than we've ever claimed," Devra objected. "You should know that best, far ranger."

Drake glared at her, at a loss for a retort. He'd spent all winter walking the longest patrol routes of the village under Devra's command and had developed a quiet, grudging respect for her.

"They're only asking for help in the short term. The first year." Amaya narrowed her eyes as she thought it through. "Grain and seeds. Potatoes. A few animals. But having another village so close as an ally could be . . . immeasurably beneficial."

The Shelter was already crowded and the outlying buildings were hard to repair and (as they'd recently discovered) unreliable. New Tacoma had the space to sprawl and the skills to build new homes as needed. Of course, that made it more vulnerable to dangers that Osto could weather easily . . .

"We need that glass," Ahmed was saying. "It would let us do so much! And if we built the mill here, we could process more wheat and corn into flour. It would help with the food shortage!"

"Of course." Amaya sighed. Ahmed had walked her through his plans for the mill months ago, and they'd both agreed that no other location was close enough to Osto to be worth it—three days of travel was already a bit much for bread and flour on an individual level, but in the broader context of the village, it helped a great deal. If they needed to find another, further location, that margin narrowed.

There was a cough from the back of the hut, and Amaya squinted through the gloom to identify one of the newcomers. Blond hair and a wide smile. What was his name? Sorsch, she thought. "We don't have to agree to give them anything. There aren't that many of them, are there? We have the numbers. And the weapons."

"Shut your mouth, idiot," Drake snapped. "We're Ostons now, and we handle this like Ostons. Understood?"

There was a long moment of quiet before the former raider nodded. Reluctantly. "Understood. Sir."

Was there an edge of mockery to his tone? Amaya gave the man a long look. She'd known of the fracture lines among the newcomers for as long as she'd been Headwoman, but so far, Drake had seemed to keep them mostly in check. The last thing she needed was for a contingent of large, violent men to decide they'd made a mistake laying down their arms.

"We aren't deciding anything yet," Amaya said, hoping she sounded more confident than she was. "We can go home with everything we've learned and talk it over as a village first. This sort of thing . . . it should be a group decision, anyway."

Confidence. Right. As though this sort of thing had ever happened before. As though there was a precedent for making decisions on this scale. What she needed was time. And distance. And to consult with Vasha.

Amaya stifled a small, slightly hysteric laugh. Would even Vasha know what to do?

". . . right," she managed, when no one answered her. "Let's go back out there and enjoy ourselves. See who else you meet and what else you can learn. Don't make any agreements yet, but . . . don't deny anything, either."

"And don't get anyone pregnant," Devra added, which drew a round of laughs and half-protests from the men as they filed out.

The last member of the delegation paused at the door, then turned and came back to her. Sarah Newsome reached for her hand. Amaya waited until she was sure the others were gone before taking it.

"You sounded good," Sarah said, her quiet voice hard to hear even in the empty hut. "Like you had a plan."

Amaya let the laugh escape this time. "Did I? Oh, good."

"Do you?"

Amaya looked away. "Not really. Not yet."

There was a beat of silence. "It would be . . . a very good thing, I think, to call these people allies."

Amaya nodded. "I think so, too."

"But we can't give away enough food to feed them all."

Amaya stilled. It was an opening, a chance to ask about the hoarded stores, the strange varietals.

A chance. But not one she would take right now. Not now. There was too much else going on to jeopardize the friendship that had come to mean so much to her, so quickly. She sighed. "I know."

Sarah nodded.

"Don't tell . . ."

She winced. "I won't. You know I won't."

". . . I know."

Jon Newsome lay in wait in the dark gulf of their unspoken words.

DAY 5

The morning dawned gray and chill, as though spring hadn't quite let go of the last pall of winter. Dew clung to the grass, cool and damp, and clouds crowded the sky. Amaya reached up and scratched her horse's broad cheek under his bridle, wondering if his disquiet was a reflection of her own. She waited in the field at the edge of town for the last few members of her party to finish their preparations for departure. A small crowd of Folk and horses gathered to see them off.

"You're welcome to stay longer, you know," Dan Tallgrass said. "We'd love to get to know our new neighbors better."

Amaya found her most polite smile for him. "Thank you for your kindness, but we really must be getting back. We need to . . . discuss things. And find an answer for you that everyone can agree on."

Dan's answering smile was tight—an uncomfortable look for his broad, friendly face. "I understand, of course. I hope you know that even if things don't work out for the best, we hope we can keep things friendly. Ostons will always be welcome here."

Amaya wondered if he could somehow read her mind—Sorsch's dour pronouncements from the night before had reminded her just how badly things could go.

"I am sure we can figure out something that will benefit both villages," she managed. "And, of course, you are welcome to come visit us. Osto is open to all."

He apparently didn't notice her hesitation on the last sentence, as he favored her again with his dazzlingly bright smile.

"And on that note! I was wondering if you might see fit to taking a few of our more curious types back with you."

"Oh?" Amaya's eyes widened in surprise.

Dan Tallgrass waved behind him, and two women stepped forward. One, tall and dark and gorgeous as the night sky, she recognized from their arrival—Grace, the villager who'd taken charge of the horses. The other woman, older and pale, walked with a practiced, easy confidence that Amaya envied.

"Grace here is one our best beast handlers, and Gemma is a glass blower."

"A master craftsman," Gemma added, with a grin and a wink that made the boast into a light tease. "I'm eager to keep talking with your George and little Ahmed."

"Ah . . ." Amaya knew she shouldn't feel so caught out, and she resented that she did. "Of course. Please, do join us. Do you . . . do you have horses?"

"All geared up, and we have road rations, too," Gemma said. "Don't worry, we won't be any burden to you."

Amaya winced and wondered if maybe some of the Oston council the previous night hadn't been as private as she'd thought. "Bring blankets and whatever else you need for the overnight, too. We'll be camping in the forest, and it gets cold out there after dark."

"Thank you, ma'am. We're used to traveling."

Amaya nodded and turned back to her horse, hoping they didn't see the blush of embarrassment at that. Of course they'd be prepared for an overnight camp. They'd been traveling their whole lives.

The stragglers of the Oston delegation congregated slowly, each in various stages of breakfast, last-minute repacking, or chatting with the locals. Gemma and Grace joined them, leading two small bay mares by braided bridles. Finally, Sorsch and another newcomer joined them, nodding quick apologies to the others for their lateness. Amaya did a quick count, just to be sure. Ten Ostons, ten horses, plus the two Folkies and their mounts. She nodded to herself, then repeated the movement more decisively and called out, "Right, then! Let's get going!"

"Home!" Devra answered, pitching it into a cheer. Several answering voices rose in agreement, and the trek began as they all, with varying degrees of skill, turned to mount their horses.

Dan Tallgrass held her horse's bridle as she mounted and handed her the reins when she was ready. "Remember what I said, Amaya Bly," he spoke up to her. "We can help each other. We all have a better chance at making it when we work together!"

Amaya nodded. "I don't disagree, Dan Tallgrass. But I don't speak for everyone, and I won't make any binding promises on my own. We'll have an answer for you when next we meet."

Dan nodded and handed her the reins, but as he turned away, his eyes seemed shadowed.

"Home!" Deetz called, and the Ostons cheered again. Amaya felt her heart lift at the thought—she had never been away from her husband and children for so long. It might still be a full day and more before she'd see Cedric, but at least they were on the downward slope now. After a quick look to ensure everyone was mounted and ready, she dug in her heels, clicked her tongue, and set her horse off at a smart trot.

The trail their arrival had broken in the tall grass of the floodplain hadn't even recovered, and they traced it back into the trees.

"Home," she whispered to herself, and sighed happily under the wide gray sky.

———

For the first time since he'd been placed under house arrest, Jon Newsome had visitors, and Jacob was having trouble making his way to his father's bedside. He tried to be polite, but the bowl of thin stew was hot even through the thick ceramic, and the burn on his fingers was becoming intolerable.

"Make way!" he called, glaring at the backs of the visitors and attempting to shoulder one aside.

His father was fully sitting up this time, his feet planted on the floor as he perched on the edge of the makeshift bed. He'd even changed clothes by himself, which was a first Jacob had given up trying to force him into something clean more than once a week. His scant hair had grown wild during his incarceration, and his skin sallow. Yet, he seemed to be holding court with ease, commanding the attention of the newcomers who had come to visit.

The small room was made close with the former raiders of Esteben's Men. Large men, muscular in ways that spoke of a life spent on activities other than farm work. Though Jacob was as tall as any of them, he still found it intimidating to face more than one of the raiders at a time. He'd spent most of the last day running messages back and forth amongst them, and now five clustered around his father's bed, variously sitting on crates or leaning against the wall, their eyes fixed on Jon Newsome with cold calculation.

The one he'd shoved barely moved. He turned to watch Jacob pick his way across the room and called, "And this one?"

"My boys are loyal," Jon said fiercely. "It's the women who ain't. But we can fix them, can't we?"

There was a general grumble of agreement. Jacob set the bowl of stew down by his father's bed and cast a dark look at the gathering. "Best not let anyone catch you all here," he said. "Pa's supposed to be kept alone."

"Lot of us don't have much use for what we're "supposed" to do," said one of the raiders, to answering dark laughter. "In fact, lot of us are gettin' sick of 'supposed to.'"

"Which is why this new village is such an opportunity," Jon answered. He leaned forward, his eyes glinting. "They've got buildings. Animals. Food. A defenseless workforce. They're just waiting for someone to come in and tell 'em how to use it."

"And that someone should be you, should it?" The speaker was a lieutenant known only as Redbane. He was freckled and tall, with arms as thick around as his neck and a shock of red hair braided close to his scalp. "Why should we listen to you, when you've failed once already?"

Jon snorted. "I didn't fail, I was betrayed. I relied on weaklings, and they broke under me. With the right allies, I'd be running this place already."

Redbane's eyes narrowed. "Awfully sure of yourself."

Jon shook his head. "You're a lieutenant, yeah? In charge of twenty men? Will they come when you call?"

"Some of 'em will still, yeah."

"Some of 'em," Jon repeated. He pinned his gaze on another newcomer sitting to his left. "And you? Will they come, lieutenant?"

This man, blond and tanned, could have been Jacob's brother. He shrugged at the question. "Some will. Some like it here, others are ready to leave."

"Same with the rest of you?" Jon demanded. He gave them each a close look, and they variously shrugged, nodded, or avoided his gaze.

"There's your answer. You're bringing some few men each with you.

I've got three sons and eight grandsons. They do as I say, don't they, boy?"

Jacob recognized this as his cue and leaped to take it. "Yes, Pa. Of course."

Jon nodded. "So, consider me another lieutenant, then. And between us, with your weapons, we should have plenty to take on this new village."

"Our weapons," Redbane repeated. "Our horses, our armor, our battle experience. Your boys are just useless bodies in a fight."

"My boys are plenty to take on a bunch of soft villagers. They don't even have a Shelter, do they?" Jon sniffed. "'Sides, we'll need the numbers to manage the survivors after the attack, won't we?"

There was a quiet, and the raiders exchanged dubious glances amongst themselves. Eventually, Redbane seemed to decide he'd been appointed as their speaker.

"It's a risk, Newsome. I may not like being told what to do by a bunch of soft farmers, but it's safe here. Clean. Warm. I'm not giving that up for a fool's gambit."

"It's safe and warm, but we ain't going to last until summer," Jon snapped. He picked up the steaming bowl of stew and waved it at the raiders. "They call this food!? We can all see how bad it is, can't we? No meat, barely anything else! I wouldn't even call it broth! Fah!"

So saying, he flung the bowl across the room. It hit the plain gray wall and shattered, large shards of ceramic and steaming liquid flying back at the men. The visitors recoiled, drawing away from the wet mess that seemed, on reflection, pitifully small.

"I'm telling you, we can have better! Our own place and people to do the work for us! It's ready and waiting; we just need to go take it!"

"Pa! They won't give you more lunch," Jacob said.

"That wasn't fit to eat," Jon growled back. "And that's the problem." His eyes were fixed on Redbane, who hadn't flinched a bit.

There was a long pause before Redbane nodded once, slow and decisive. "It's an interesting proposition, Newsome. But it's too much to risk, and you're not someone I'd lay my money on. For now, we stay with Osto. C'mon, Men."

So saying, he turned and started from the room.

"Osto will not reward your loyalty!" Jon cried. He stood up even as the others started following Redbane out. "You'll see! The Headwoman will lead us to ruin, and you'll die knowing you had the chance to get out!"

The last of the lieutenants, the blond one, paused at the door and looked back at Jon with a strangely thoughtful air. "Give it time," he said, his voice low and carrying. "You're not wrong. When things get bad, this place will turn on us. Then they'll see."

"Pfauh!" Jon cried, and for a second, he looked tempted to throw something else. With nothing in reach, he instead fell back onto the bed. The raider was already gone, the door closing behind him.

". . . sorry, Pa," Jacob ventured. It had been good, for just a moment, to see the spark back in his father's eyes.

"Don't you 'sorry' me, boy. Clean that up," Jon snapped. So saying, he lay on the bed and turned his back on the room.

———

It had been a very long time since she'd slept under the stars. Amaya found herself torn—she very much wanted to stare into the fire or up at the sky and think about the last time she'd huddled close against the dark, so many years ago, but now she had responsibilities—too many to let herself get distracted. As much as her memories plucked at the edges of her consciousness, she forced herself to stay present, alert, and aware of the people around her.

Or so she thought. Even as she forced her mind back to the present, a body seemed to appear from the darkness and sat down beside her with a heavy grunt, almost a fall. She squinted in the firelight and was relieved to realize it was only Sarah. Sweet Sarah, who would surely understand if she did not feel like answering too many questions.

"Hungry?" Sarah held out a steaming bundle wrapped in cloth. Amaya took it gratefully—a roasted potato, pulled straight from the coals only a few minutes before. She unwrapped it and broke it open, watching the heat curl up from the starchy insides, feeling again that tug of memory.

"Thank you. I take it the fish isn't ready yet?" she said.

Sarah waved the question away. "I've had enough fish. Haven't you? Besides, this way, we can save some for the village."

Amaya nodded at that and blew on her tuber.

"So . . ."

"So." Sarah arched an eyebrow at her.

Amaya sighed. Might as well cut to the chase. "What do you think of New Tacoma?"

Sarah pursed her lips and looked away. Her answer, when it came, carried some of the hesitancy she'd been working so hard to shed over the last six months. "I'm . . . not sure. They seem like good people. I want to help them. And it would be the right thing to do. But . . ."

"But you're not sure if helping them would wind up hurting us."

Sarah nodded. "You know better than I what our stores look like. Can we give them what they're asking for?"

"No."

Sarah's eyes widened. "Then why are we even talking about it? Why didn't you just tell them that?"

"It's not that simple." Amaya frowned, trying to marshal her thoughts. "If we gave them everything they are asking for, they'd be eating better than we are now, and we'd be starving. We can't do that. But we could work something else out—something that would help us both survive until harvest time."

Sarah tilted her head. "Like what?"

That was the tricky part, wasn't it? "Well . . . if Ahmed and George can get their mill going, we'll be able to make flour faster. More risen loaves, and more time for people to do other things, like hunting or scavenging."

"But that's a different problem." Sarah's eyes were fixed on Amaya, measuring her reaction. "We're worried now about having enough grain, not how fast we can turn it into flour. And besides, that mill will take months to build, won't it?"

"If the Folkies even let us," Amaya agreed. She sighed and took a bite of her potato to delay the need to answer. It was still too hot, and she sucked in a mouthful of cool night air to try to avoid burning her mouth. "For now, if both villages pool our resources, we might be able to do it. We can hunt more, slaughter more of the goats and chickens than we planned—"

"More jerky?" Sarah wrinkled her nose.

"Fish jerky would be a change?" Amaya offered with half a grin, and when Sarah's expression deepened, they both ended up laughing.

When they sobered up, Amaya found herself giving Sarah a sidelong glance and thinking back to her last conversation with Vasha. Surely, if anything was going to convince Sarah she no longer needed to fear Jon . . . "We might look at trading, if any more travelers come through," she started, trying to be delicate. "I know there's . . . different varieties of vegetables out there that we don't have. Maybe we could start new fields. See if any of them grow faster than what we have."

Sarah was quiet at that. Amaya wanted to give her friend the chance to come around to it on her own, but she couldn't quite let it sit. The hoarded food sat between them, invisible, unacknowledged, impossible to ignore. "Do you . . . ?"

"We have too many people already," Sarah said suddenly. "We can't just keep taking in more."

Amaya blinked. "We're not taking in anyone. This would be a temporary arrangement, a donation for the year, and next year, both villages will be better off and independent."

"That's what we thought last summer," Sarah said, an edge of bitterness in her tone. "Remember? It was the best harvest ever. Winter was supposed to be easy and comfortable, for once. This year was supposed to be easy. Finally. But then we suddenly had the newcomers."

"Sarah . . ." *You sound like Jon.* No. She absolutely could not say that. "We're Oston. We have a duty to help people—"

"We have a duty to help *each other*! To protect ourselves!" Sarah's voice went loud and high, enough to be clearly audible over at the campfire. Both women waited, tense, to see if anyone came over in response, but no one did.

Amaya frowned at her friend. They had come far together over the last six months, from reluctant allies to fast friends. Amaya knew—or thought she knew—Sarah's mind almost as well as her own. The woman was clever, determined, and fiercely protective of her children, even those who had not followed her into the Shelter. But Sarah bore scars from her long marriage to Jon Newsome, thought patterns she sometimes didn't realize she still fell into. Fears that troubled her dreams, even if she banished them from her waking mind.

When Sarah had volunteered to come on the expedition, neither of them had needed to voice that Jon Newsome was in the Shelter now, all too close for her fragile peace of mind.

"Sarah," Amaya said softly. "What is it?"

Sarah looked away. The firelight played over her face, creating planes of shadow and light.

Moments passed. When she spoke, it was almost too quiet to hear. Amaya leaned forward.

"Gabrielle's pregnant."

The news flashed through her like lightning. Amaya gasped as a hundred thoughts crashed through her head at once. Gabrielle was—!? Then Umair—! That meant—

"I'm going to be a grandmother?!"

Sarah's laugh this time had an edge to it. "Just two nosy old grannies, that's us."

"Umair didn't tell me!"

"Umair doesn't know yet." Sarah's eyes widened. "And . . . and please don't tell him. Let Gaby work her way to it when she's ready."

The implications of *that* were not lost on her at any stretch. Even so, Amaya took a few moments to savor the news, letting the pure joy of it wash over her.

"I have to tell Cedric."

Sarah ducked her head in acknowledgment. "He can keep a secret. Better than I can, I guess."

"Ha!"

But the reminder was a sobering one. Amaya stared at the fire as her mind raced back over the previous conversation.

"You're worried for your grandchild?"

"I'm worried for Gabrielle. And Umair. And all of us. If Osto keeps growing—if we give away all that we have—what will be left for us?" Sarah shook her head. "Jon . . . talked a lot about looking out for ourselves first. I mean, I know it's not very Oston, but when you hear it enough, it does start to make sense. He even had us growing our own supplies, separate from the village."

Amaya blinked at the casual admission to the very crime she'd been worrying over. "Ah . . ."

"You must have found the stores by now. I know you had Stan looking at the house."

Amaya felt her cheeks flush in a strange embarrassment. "I wasn't sure how to bring it up."

Sarah shrugged. "I can show you where it is. Might as well. It isn't enough to feed two villages, though. Just one small patch, back in the forest."

"Sarah. You have to know I won't let anything happen to the children. Especially not our grandbaby."

"I'm not—it's not about you, though." Sarah gave Amaya a frank look. "I know you have the best of intentions. I know you'll look out for us all. That's why I voted for you."

"Then . . ." Amaya bit her lip. It was difficult, asking for something she wasn't entirely certain she had earned. "Then trust me. Please. Let me figure this out. For all of us."

In the dim light this far from the fire, Sarah's blue eyes danced with sparks. "I . . . I will. I do."

Amaya nodded and took another bite of her potato. It was cool enough, this time.

DAY 6

Anton Johnson was not hiding. Hiding was for children's games, and he was not a child and most certainly not playing a game.

No, he told himself. He was up on the roof of the Shelter, where almost no one went, to check on the progress of Ahmed's garden in his absence. He'd volunteered for the job, and he was doing it very, very carefully.

There was little to see, just yet. Just as there had been little to see yesterday, when he hadn't been hiding before. Or the day before that. Or the day before that, when he'd watched Amaya and Ahmed and George and the others ride out to greet the strangers. The newcomers. The other village.

He wrenched his thoughts away from that particular abyss and forced himself to focus on the garden. Plots of rich black soil, carefully harvested from the floodplain of the creek behind the Shelter. Tall supports of stick and string set up and waiting to be called into use. Long, shallow tubs of water, for what purpose he couldn't guess.

Most of the garden was empty, so early in the season. More an idea than a garden, really. Potential, like a collection of carefully wound skeins of yarn, waiting to be threaded onto a loom.

In one plot, a single tiny seedling poked through the surface of the loamy soil. Anton reached out to touch a fingertip to the delicate green leaves and paused as his hand shook.

A newcomer. Maybe not all newcomers are bad.

Just briefly, he smiled.

A strange sound broke through his reverie. It was quiet enough at first that he thought he had to be imagining it, but soon enough, the source was plain—a group of weary horses and their riders approached the Shelter from across the plaza. Anton suppressed a flash of terror at the sight as he leaned over the edge of the roof and forced himself to identify the riders. There was George. Where was Ahmed? There was Devra. Sarah Newsome. There—

He blinked. Two strangers rode with the group, neither Oston nor newcomer.

And the *colors* on those strangers! Periwinkle on the older woman, rich and subtle. Brilliant, vivid orange on the younger, paired with a head wrap in alternating stripes of blue and orange—he was too far away to determine the weave, but was it even possible it was a print? Painted? He leaned further, trying to get a better look, and nearly fell off the roof.

Where did they find such pigments?

Anton caught his breath, wondering at the sudden burst of curiosity. He wanted to go downstairs and get a better look at those textiles. He wanted to talk to the strangers, hear about their pigments and their dye methods. He wanted to see how they kept the colors so bright. He wanted . . .

He blinked for a moment.

I want to see what's out there.

———

Gabrielle was delaying the inevitable, she knew. She had signed up for a full day of hunting duties because they were the only free assignment that would allow her to avoid speaking to anyone, but after a fruitless morning, she had to admit her heart wasn't in it—this would be a day wasted. She had returned to the village, ready to change out for whatever spare duty might still be open for the afternoon, but found herself reluctant to face anyone. Instead, she lingered behind the new horse barn, leaning against the rough wood and staring into the encroaching forest. The newcomers meant to clear out some of the growth around the barn to make a paddock, but for now, the trees marched right up to the back of the building, and the branches dipped down to brush against the roof like the living wood paid tribute to the dead.

"Oh! I'm sorry!"

Gabrielle jumped at the words—she hadn't heard anyone approaching—perhaps a measure of how far away her thoughts were. She jumped again when she spotted the speaker—a tall, thin, dark-skinned woman she had never seen before in her life.

"Oh! You are . . . ?" Gabrielle glanced around, wondering if there were other strangers surrounding her, wondering if she were suddenly in danger.

"Sorry again. I'm Grace. From New Tacoma." The stranger had a brilliant wide smile and a soft gravel to her voice that soothed.

Gabrielle blinked.

"The, uh, the other village. By the river."

"Oh! My mom went out there. Are they—I guess they're back?" Gabrielle had to work to pull her thoughts back to the present, to calm her breathing from the sudden rush of fear. Her mother! She'd missed her deeply, even in the mere three days of her absence.

"They are, yes. And a few of us came back with them to see Osto. I was told I could see all your horses here. And other animals?"

"Someone should be showing you around," Gabrielle said, frowning. Then she shrugged. "I guess I can. You want to go inside?"

Grace brightened. "Sure!"

Gabrielle pasted on a smile. This, at least, she could handle. Someone should have been accompanying Grace already. She'd just take that on herself. It would be a good distraction from . . . other issues. And Grace wouldn't know enough about her or her family to know she was avoiding anything in particular.

"This all looks new," Grace was saying. "Did you keep all the horses in the big building before?"

"Oh, no . . ." Gabrielle waved her toward the front of the building. "We didn't have horses before last winter. You didn't hear about that?"

"About what?"

Gabrielle paused, wondering where to start. "What do you know about Osto?"

"Not more than what anyone knows, really," Grace shrugged. "You're a safe and kind place that welcomes anyone."

"Heh. Well." Gabrielle couldn't help but compare that description to her father's derisive opinions. "We do welcome anyone. And last summer, we welcomed over a hundred new people all at once. They brought horses. And more."

"A hundred!" Grace gave an astonished laugh. "You could do that?!"

"Well . . . we don't know, yet," Gabrielle answered, looking away. "Vasha thought so. Amaya thinks so."

"Oh." They stopped short of the barn's front door, and Grace turned to her. "You don't?"

Gabrielle froze at the question. She hadn't quite committed her thoughts to such solid form as words just yet. "I . . . don't know. I used to."

"Before you actually lived it?" Grace's tone was extremely soft.

Gabrielle looked away. The truth wasn't quite that stark, not really. She was committed to the Oston way—she always had been, despite her father's views. But it was easy to commit herself alone to the trials of a lean winter and an uncertain future—it was different when she had another life to look out for. Unconsciously, she moved to rest a hand on her belly, then caught the movement and instead pushed the barn door open. "Some of the horses will be out on patrol rounds, but most of them should be here."

Grace gave her a long look but seemed to accept the change of subject and preceded her into the barn. Her gasp of delight was a gratifying confirmation that the tactic had worked.

"So many! And so fine! What do you feed them?"

Gabrielle followed her in and left the door open for the light. "I'm not really the one to ask, honestly. You'd have to talk to Devra for that. Or one of the newcomers."

"Devra was in the delegation," Grace said. She was already holding her hand out to the nearest horse with her head out of her stall, a large chestnut mare who sniffed greedily at her palm. "Are the newcomers the ones in all the leather?"

That surprised a snort of laughter from Gabrielle. "That's them," she agreed.

"That won't be very practical in the summer," Grace said. "You'll be needing to find a hundred people's worth of field clothes."

"Ah . . ." Gabrielle frowned. Did this woman think she knew everything about how Osto was run? "I'm sure someone's working on that."

"Mm. Or no one's thought of it yet, and you'll get a bunch of people trying to plant fields in leather armor."

"My da would say it was an insult to expect warriors to farm."

Grace raised an eyebrow. "Your da doesn't sound very Oston."

"I . . . I'm not supposed to talk to him anymore," Gabrielle admitted. This time, she couldn't stop her hand from resting on her belly, feeling the slight swelling there.

Grace watched her with keen, bright eyes. "Can I ask . . . how does Osto deal with people who don't sound Oston?"

"That's . . ." The gasp surprised her, catching at her throat and threatening to close it.

"Gabrielle?"

Gabrielle shook her head quickly. There was no way she could share everything going on—both in the village and inside her—with a complete stranger. "I'm sorry. It's really not something for you to worry about. Really."

Grace gave her a long look at that. The mare, realizing she probably wasn't going to get any treats out of the interaction, gave a soft whuff and withdrew into her stall.

"I know I'm no one to you," Grace said, her voice low. "But sometimes, no one is the best person you can talk to, if you need to. So, you know. If you need to talk, I'm happy to listen."

Gabrielle shivered. The offer was certainly tempting, but there was simply too much—too much she would have to explain, too much history she could never fully convey to one who didn't live through it all herself.

"You're . . . you're very kind," she managed.

Grace sighed at that, closing her eyes briefly before opening them with a wide smile. "What I am is too nosy for my own good, I expect. I'm sorry. Why don't you tell me more about these horses?"

"I don't really know much about them," Gabrielle said. "I'm sorry. I'm really not the best guide, am I?"

"Oh. Well . . ." Grace gave the barn a disappointed look. "Why don't you show me something you do know well, then?"

"I . . ." She really didn't want to see people. She couldn't face Umair right now, not to mention his parents. Everyone would be rushing around welcoming back the delegation, dealing with the visitors, exchanging gossip and rumors. Her mother would probably be too busy to talk to her for hours yet.

"Gabrielle?" Grace asked. Her eyes were wide and soft and so very kind.

Gabrielle shook her head, and before she knew it, the whole sordid story was spilling out of her—her father's hatred, her mother's suffering, her and Umair and their decision to flee, her hesitation that had driven them to turn back. Then the discovery of the raiders and everything that came after. In the isolation of the barn, under the gentle concern of a total stranger, the looming fears she'd been trying so hard to keep at bay at last found their outlet, and Grace learned more than she'd ever expected to about the current state of Osto.

Later, much later, as Grace hugged her and Gabrielle had managed to harness her breathing, Grace ventured, ". . . You know. You and Umair. The Blys and the Newsomes. You're like Romeo and Juliet."

Gabrielle let a few moments pass in near silence before she managed, "Who are they?"

Grace gave a soft laugh. "Who *were* they, you mean. If they were ever real. You haven't heard of Shakespeare?"

Gabrielle shook her head. "Is that someone's name? Like a raider?"

This time, the laugh was louder. "No, no! Very much the opposite of a raider, in fact."

Gabrielle stayed quiet, waiting for Grace to fill in the blanks, and Grace eventually realized it.

"William Shakespeare was a writer, long, long ago. Five hundred years ago."

"The old world," Gabrielle supplied. In her head, she heard Pa's derisive snort for anything so soft as writing.

"Right, but not just the old world. Before what we would have known as the old world. Before all the trouble started, William Shakespeare wrote a play called Romeo and Juliet."

"A play's when people act things out for you," Gabrielle said. "We do that sometimes here, when the light stays long enough and the work is done. I like the funny ones."

"Right, that's right." Grace's smile was bright in the dim light. "But these were longer plays that were written down so the same story could be told by different people all over the world. Shakespeare's were the best. No one wrote like him. And Romeo and Juliet is his most romantic story."

"Oh yeah?" Gabrielle smiled, curious. She didn't much think about romance, but Umair did say the sweetest things sometimes, and early in their courtship, he'd lent her a book of poetry that nearly took her breath away.

"Oh, it's beautiful, Gabrielle. Two families, constantly at war, but the daughter from one and the son from the other fall in love. 'Two houses, both alike in circumstance . . .' If you ever come to New Tacoma, you can read it. We have all of Shakespeare's works."

"We're trying not to be at war anymore," Gabrielle objected. "Amaya and Cedric are very nice to us."

"There's more to the story than that! It's about *romance*." Grace waved the objection away. "It's about love overcoming everything and healing two broken houses. It's about how feuds and families mean nothing in the face of true love. Listen!"

Grace struck a pose, closed her eyes, and took a moment to compose herself. When she spoke, her words came out measured and calm, yet her voice shook as though she were holding back some great wave of emotion.

"What's Montague? It is nor hand nor foot
Nor arm nor face nor any other part
Belonging to a man. O be some other name.
What's in a name? That which we call a rose
By any other name would smell as sweet;
So Romeo would, were he not Romeo call'd,
Retain that dear perfection which he owes
Without that title. Romeo, doff thy name,
And for that name, which is no part of thee,
Take all myself."

Grace finished the recitation by laying a hand on her heart and gazing up into the rafters above them.

Gabrielle smiled, more taken by the performance than the words. "That was beautiful."

"You should hear the whole thing someday." Grace grinned. "Or read it, like I said. Or watch it. Maybe things will calm down enough, once we're all settled, that we can actually try to perform it!"

Gabrielle's eyes widened. "My father would hate that."

Mischief washed across Grace's face. "All the more reason to do it then, right?"

———

"Hey. Your dad seeing visitors?"

Jacob looked up in surprise. No one other than his own brothers had talked to him for days, and with the return of the delegation from the other village, he had thought he'd be alone in his efforts to scavenge through the remains of the Newsome home. He didn't expect to find anything left in the rubble, but no one much questioned him about his desire to look, and it gave him an excuse to get away from the Shelter and his father dwelling within it.

The speaker was one of the newcomers—a tall man with short blond hair. Jacob vaguely recognized him as one of those who had gone to the other village.

He dropped the wood scraps he'd been examining and stood up straight. "No one's supposed to talk to him. He's under house arrest."

"Yeah, I know. But is he?"

Jacob hesitated. The answer was yes, obviously, but no one was supposed to know that.

"Some friends of mine have been saying some real interesting things about your dad," the newcomer continued. "Some things that sound a lot like things I've been thinking. I just want to see if they're true."

It had been one thing to sneak people in to see Pa when the Headwoman was out of town, and everyone else was busy with their own worries. Now that everyone was back, the Shelter would be busier than ever. Which hardly mattered, of course, since no one was supposed to talk to Pa at all, according to Vasha and Amaya.

But then, if Pa ever found out he'd refused someone like this, there wouldn't be much left of him for Amaya to punish.

"Door to his room is in the back, near the women's lots," Jacob said. He spoke quietly, even though no one else was around. "Go in through the animal pens and keep close to the wall. Don't let anyone see you go in."

"Is the door locked?"

He hesitated. "Yes."

"You got a key?"

This was his chance to refuse and keep Pa from making another mistake. Who knew what they would do to him this time?

Who knew what Pa would do to him?

Jacob sighed. "Yes."

DAY 7

ama."

It was amazing how tone of voice alone could convey the importance of the topic someone wished to discuss. Sarah had just been about to leave the family allotment, ready to drop off the breakfast dishes at the kitchens before checking in on the infirmary, but she checked her regret and turned back to face Gabrielle. The girl must have been waiting for just this moment—Eric had already left for his morning duties, and the Bly lot next door was silent.

Which was perfect because they had things to discuss.

"How are you holding up, heart?"

Gabrielle shook her head. "I . . . I don't know. It's a lot. I suppose I should be trying to get used to it."

"Gabrielle." Sarah took a deep breath. "The other village—the Folk—they have medicines we don't. They—well, Fantra, the one they call Nana, she has so much we could learn."

"I know, Mom. And it'll be good to learn from them." Gabrielle gave her a curious look. "I'm sure we have medicines they could use, too."

"Yes, of course. But I'm talking specifically." Another deep breath. Her heart was pounding hard, the way it always did when she knew Jon would be angry. Lately, she'd come to recognize it as a sign she was doing the right thing. Sarah took her daughter's hands and gave them a squeeze. "Specifically, Gabrielle. They know—she knows—you don't have to be pregnant if you don't want to."

There was a beat of silence, of stillness. Sarah watched as Gabrielle processed the news. She watched—she was sure—as the girl quietly went through the same litany of remembered tragedy, the same missing family members that she had.

"It's . . . it's safe?" Gabrielle asked. "And certain?"

Sarah nodded. "So long as it's early enough. It's basically a tea—she gave me some. And she promised to share some seedlings with us once they've got their gardens established, so we'll be able to grow our own."

"I could end it." Gabrielle blinked down at her stomach, still flat despite what she knew to be happening within.

"No one else has to know," Sarah said. "And you'll be able to conceive when you decide you're ready—you and Umair both."

"That's . . ." Gabrielle shook her head, still grappling with the idea.

"It's choice, dear heart. It's… it's freedom. Freedom to decide your own path in life."

Gabrielle took a deep breath, hard and fast. Her eyes shone bright with sudden, unshed tears. "Choice. Yes."

Sarah pushed on quickly. "Whatever you decide, I'll support it. I'll support you. You don't have to do anything you don't want to, understand me?"

Sarah swallowed the rest of her words. Because that was it, wasn't it? That was the important part. Gabrielle could have something she'd never had—and it wasn't even really about Fantra and her herbs. It wasn't about population growth or resources or family dynamics. It was about choice—Gabrielle's choice, hers and hers alone. It was about being able to live her life free from her father's toxic influence, free from his mandates, free from his warped ideas about women and children and family.

Gabrielle shouldn't have to do anything she didn't want to do, and now she didn't have to.

———

Amaya should have expected this. She'd called the meeting; she'd left it open to all who wished to attend—even granted a pass on daily duty rotation. So, she should have expected that half the village would show up, all eager to hear the details and offer their opinions on this most unprecedented event. The crowd filled the communal space at the front of the Shelter, leaning against walls or sitting on whatever they'd dragged out of their allotments. They made a wide, rough circle focused on the counters and tall stools of the kitchens where Amaya was sitting. She had shooed Old Ben and his friends out for the moment, though they had just dragged their normal stools to the side and sat there now, creating a formidable wall of aged wisdom. Vasha had joined the other old-timers, though she sat behind them as though deliberately positioning herself out of the spotlight. Danica, Lani, and even little Chloe sat beside them, though Chloe was not best pleased with Lani's attempts to make her sit still and quiet.

Grace and Gemma, the two visiting Folkies, were the only other people seated at the kitchen counters—a place of honor that, coincidentally, made them easily visible to all curious eyes.

Across the circle, the outlying Newsomes lurked, quiet and uncertain. Sour men and quiet women, with a gaggle of teenagers who looked like they'd rather be anywhere else. They'd lost the simmering anger that had so long seemed to drive the family, the air of incipient offense that so many of them had carried with them wherever they'd gone. Maybe it was the missing members that had left the family fractured—Jon Newsome was conspicuous by his absence, and Sarah, Gabrielle, and Eric sat with Amaya's own family.

Amaya found herself seeking out Cedric and the kids, and tried to take comfort in his big, confident grin.

Even with the front doors of the Shelter wide open, it felt close and crowded. Or maybe that was just her nervousness. The last field hand had left the building five minutes ago. There were no more stragglers coming. She was just delaying now, putting off the inevitable.

Wasting time.

"Well," she muttered to herself. She plastered on a smile and raised her voice to include Grace and Gemma as she said, "I guess we'd better get on with it."

They gave her answering smiles, though Gemma looked a bit bewildered, and Grace seemed to be straight up overwhelmed.

Amaya stood up, and the scrape of her stool rang loud in the Shelter, silencing the wave of whispered speculation.

"As you know by now," she started, too soft, and then tried again, louder. "As you know by now, we have new neighbors, and three days ago, we met them for the first time. The Folklife Department of the University of Washington, known as New Tacoma, has settled on the riverbank a day and a half north of us."

There was a rush of reaction from the crowd, curiosity and restlessness combined. No shouted questions just yet—they were all waiting for her to offer more information without prompting.

"New Tacoma is rich in culture and history. There's a lot we can learn from them—crafts that have been lost to us for decades. This alliance could be beneficial to both villages. We'd reap benefits from it we can't even understand yet."

This time, the rustle of response was more positive, she thought. Gentle surprise, curiosity, and relief. Not a bad place to start an alliance.

"With us today are Grace and Gemma, two Folkies who volunteered to come back with us and share a little more about the history and specialties of their village."

There was a rapt silence as Gemma stepped forward. The woman was an apt representative of her people—tall, tanned, and wiry; only a few lines around her sharp dark eyes and her shock of cropped gray hair gave away her age. She took a slow look around the room, and Amaya was certain that she was taking stock of every single person there, sussing out relationships, weighing responses, missing nothing.

"Hello," she said. "My name's Gemma. I'm a glassblower and a smith. I'm looking forward to helping Osto get set up with its own kiln. I was born in the Folklife caravan, and I'd be happy to answer any questions you might have about it."

There was a moment of silence. Then, incredibly, Stan Johnson raised his hand like he was still a boy in classes. The crowd was quiet for the moment, content to let Stan set the tone.

Gemma gave him a warm smile. "Yes?"

"It's always a pleasure to meet other good folks," Stan started. He stood with one hand on his son Anton's shoulder. "And beg pardon that this doesn't sound too suspicious. But are we really supposed to believe that in all the wide world out there, you just happened to settle close to us? By accident?"

"Oh! No, not at all!" Gemma blinked in surprise. "Part of it was forced, of course. We were trying to avoid the fires of the south, and the sour winds of the west are getting worse. Part of it was a search for resources. This area was once famous for its glasswork, and we're hoping we can find the sands they used to use around here. But part of it is also . . . well, everyone's heard of Osto. We were hoping to find friends."

There was another moment of quiet at this, and Amaya found herself searching the faces of her fellow Ostons, looking for any clue as to how they were taking this. Some, she was certain, seemed to be exchanging slightly shame-faced, guilty looks. The outlying Newsomes were holding back, their expressions blank and unreadable.

Another farmer raised her hand and Gemma looked slightly amused as she said, "Yes?"

"No one here will turn away new friends," said the woman. "And we'll always be happy to trade for crops as we don't have yet. But why give us a kiln? Why not keep that for yourself? Glass goods are rare in trade."

"But that's the point. They don't have to be!" Gemma answered almost before the woman was finished talking. "With proper glass jars, more food can be saved and stored over the winter! Preserves have saved my people more than once over the years. Having more food available can only benefit everyone. What kind of neighbors would we be if we withheld that kind of help?"

"And you don't want anything in exchange for it?" Someone called the question from the far side of the circle.

Gemma paused at that, and offered a strained smile. "This may sound strange to you, but I don't want to be the only glassblower in the world. In New Tacoma, we believe the best way to preserve skills and crafts is to spread them as widely as possible. We're always looking to share what we know."

Several people in the crowd gave incredulous snorts while a few more called out questions. Amaya sensed the discussion turning tense and decided it was time to step in.

"It's true," she said, raising her voice. Gratifyingly, the crowd quieted to hear her. "It's true that they have offered to share their crafts with us without price. Not just glassworking, but others, too. Weaving and dying techniques, and seeds for textiles we aren't familiar with. It's a truly generous offer."

She paused, and noted again that expectant, waiting silence. "It is also true that they have asked us for a gift of food and grain to see them through their first year or so of settlement."

The response was instant, and far louder than any of the previous rumblings of the crowd. Every farmer present roared a denial, only too aware of how low their grain stores had dropped over the winter. Even a few of the oldtimers who minded the kitchens and thus knew full well what their food options had been for the last few months gave startled protests. Amaya waited for the first reaction to spend itself, then raised her hand.

"Before you all form any opinions, be aware that New Tacoma is much smaller than Osto, and we have taken in bigger groups before."

"Recently! Very recently!" someone called, to a surge of supportive responses.

"We haven't made any decisions yet," Amaya raised her voice for the first time. "I was hoping a part of this meeting could be a discussion of how we could each help each other."

"Haven't we helped enough strangers already?" someone called. This brought another surge of response, though it wasn't strictly supportive. A few of the newcomers were frowning darkly at the implicit reference.

"All the glass jars in the world won't help if we don't have anything to put in them!" This was almost certainly from a Newsome.

"We can't." This was Stan Johnson, and again, the crowd quieted to let him speak. "We can't give up any of our seed grain, Amaya. We'll fall short, even with the best summer possible."

The crowd gave a soft grumble of agreement, but the eruption of anger seemed to have passed.

"We're also offering food!" Grace, quiet until now, jumped from her stool to face the crowd, her head held high. "We fish and hunt ourselves, and we know all the edible plants! We have stored preserves! We're not just asking you to give up your stores. We are offering you some of everything we have and only ask that you help us survive. Please. Please . . ."

Grace turned to Gemma and Amaya, her eyes wide. Gemma nodded quickly and came to the girl's side, putting an arm around her in reassurance.

"We will understand if you can't," Gemma said, her low voice carrying through the quiet. "And our offer doesn't depend on this. We will teach and share what we have. Always. It's so important. You must know we all have a better chance of surviving if we work together!"

The silence, this time, was thick with unspoken disagreement. Amaya scanned the faces of her fellow Ostons, trying to gauge the mood of the room and the general balance of understanding against argument. She saw uncertainty, worry, and tension in nearly everyone, but no one —not even the Newsomes—seemed like they wanted to speak against such sentiment.

Vasha sat back, well out of the circle of villagers. Their eyes met, and Amaya let herself hope that the former Headwoman, loved and respected for so many years, would speak up on behalf of the nascent alliance.

Vasha raised her eyebrows. A single, small gesture, nearly invisible in the dimly lit building. That was it.

Amaya's stomach sank. If even Vasha wouldn't speak in support of the alliance, how was she supposed to make any of this work?

Stan Johnson, seemingly self-elected speaker for the farmers, cleared his throat. "Why don't we offer them whatever's left after planting?"

Amaya blinked, but before she could marshal a response, the discussion was already out of her hands.

Someone near her called, "There won't be anything left after planting. We'll be lucky if we even manage to sow all the fields."

"You can't know that," said a third.

"I've been farming these fields my whole life. I know how much seed we need!"

"And that was before the newcomers showed up!"

There was a general rumble of agreement.

"That's an empty promise and a paltry offering." The remonstration, clear and firm and certain, silenced the crowd as everyone turned to stare.

It was Sarah Newsome who raised her chin, defiant in the face of half the village's surprise. "You can't claim to offer an open hand and not put anything in it. That's no way to start a friendship. We're Osto. We need to act like it."

There was a quiet at that, as a hundred villagers weighed their shame against their hard-won practicality.

Amaya couldn't help but notice that, though they did not participate in the argument, the newcomers present seemed to have a range of reactions of their own. They were silent in the face of the sideways slights against their presence; throughout the winter, they'd shown admirable restraint in response to resentment. But even so, a split was obvious amongst them. Some scowled darkly at the arguments against the offering. Others kept their faces carefully blank and seemed to be taking note of who fell on which side of the debate.

"We can't just give all our resources away to every open hand that shows up," Stan said at last. "We need to consider our own survival. We can't *be* Osto if we all die of starvation."

"We can't be Osto if we refuse aid when it is requested," Sarah replied, her soft drawl underscoring her words.

Amaya had never been prouder of her friend. She tried to sneak a look at the rest of the Newsome clan and saw only sullen resentment on the faces of the adults. The younger members, though, the young wives and teenagers who had presumably chafed under Jonathan's rule, seemed to wear expressions of carefully guarded hope as they watched.

Amaya cleared her throat. "Let's adjourn," she said. "You've all brought up some excellent points, and we'll have to work toward a solution that satisfies everyone. Including the Folk. Please make Grace and Gemma feel welcome for the rest of their stay, and don't hesitate to approach any of us with ideas or proposals for how we can . . . how we can ensure both villages have bright futures."

It was a good closing statement, she felt. Gently chiding, but still open to all ideas. Now she only needed an excuse to seek shelter from all the staring, accusing eyes. She took a deep breath, smiled at Grace and Gemma, and nodded at Sarah. "Have you had a chance to see our infirmary yet? I'd love to know what you think."

True to her name, Grace inclined her head regally, as though there weren't a hundred people watching them both closely. "We'd love to."

"Great! This way, please."

Amaya kept the steel in her spine long after they passed through the Shelter doors.

———

Dinner that night was nothing special, but it felt different to Gabrielle, somehow, with Grace by her side. Old Ben and his helpers had served up a stew thick with root vegetables and new spring greens, with a few scant shreds of fish contributed by the New Tacoman delegation. The Bly allotment was crowded at the best of times since they'd basically taken in Gabrielle and her Ma and brother, but it was a cozy place. With Grace added to the supper circle, there was very little room to spare.

Gabrielle cradled her empty bowl close to her body and sneaked a glance around the group. Ma, Eric, Umair, Amaya, Cedric, and Umair's sisters Reggie and Jess did their best to be polite to their guests as they ate. But strangers were a rare and precious event in Osto, and little Jess was full-on staring, her dinner forgotten, drinking in Grace's every move.

"And where are you from?"

Grace finished swallowing and smiled. "We're called the Folklife Department of the University of Washington."

"But where?"

"Well, Washington was a state out on the west coast of the country—"

"The west coast? Where all the fires are?"

"There are a lot of fires," Grace agreed, solemnly. "And there's not much drinkable water. And there used to be a lot of fighting. That's why we—well, my parents and their friends—left."

"Why aren't there fires here?" Jess asked. Then, a half-second later, she followed up with, "Is it because we have more water?"

"That's certainly part of it," Cedric said, smiling at his daughter. "But not all. We've told you how we used to live in a cafila on the plains to the south? We had fire weather there, too."

"But not here?" Jess asked, and Reggie nodded vigorously, seconding the question.

"Not here," Cedric confirmed.

"Why not?"

Gabrielle smiled, only half listening as the Blys deftly distracted the younger kids from their rudeness. Umair looked just as taken with their tales of the old days as the kids, and Ma and Eric seemed to listen politely as they ate. In fact, she and Grace were the only ones who weren't listening, and somehow, she wasn't surprised when Grace leaned over until their shoulders touched.

"Gabrielle, would you show me the other animals?" she asked, loudly enough to interrupt the others.

"Oh . . . sure." Gabrielle blinked and put her bowl in the center of the circle, where there'd eventually be a pile of empty dishes to be taken to the kitchens. "Now?"

"If that's okay."

"I guess they should all be in for the night . . ." Gabrielle shot her mom a guilty look, but Sarah only nodded, smiling slightly.

"If you see Devra, let her know I'd like to talk to her?" Amaya asked.

"Yes, ma'am. Of course." Gabrielle constrained her instinctive urge to curtsey as she stood. She couldn't quite manage to address the Headwoman with anything less than high formality, even though they'd been neighbors for months.

"Thank you," Amaya said, turning back to the littles to continue the story.

"The pens are in the back," Gabrielle told Grace. She grabbed a lantern as she left the lot, leading their guest out of the family section. The allotments were a maze of high curtains and scavenged patchwork fences, marking out a makeshift labyrinth throughout the interior of the Shelter. Though she'd lived there as a child, the Newsomes had moved to their outlying home long enough ago that the lots had shifted from her memory. As a result, Gabrielle still had to navigate by landmark and memorize directions—a stark contrast to the Ostons, who had grown up in the lots and could find their way with their eyes closed no matter how things changed. Luckily, it was still early enough that most families had candles and lanterns lit, providing a consistent glow of illumination as the village ate dinner and settled for the evening. They meandered through the lots until Gabrielle realized she should be at least attempting to explain things.

"These are the women's quarters." She waved an arm, trying to encompass the entire sprawl in front of them. The women's quarters took up half the back row of the Shelter, stretching from one side to the other in a patchwork of blankets, curtains, and scavenged wood. They were generally larger than the family allotments but more crowded— each of the women's rooms contained two sets of bunk beds, an assortment of seating, and some form of storage for each inhabitant. Opposite the lots, the back wall of the Shelter was interrupted by only a few doors—one to the livestock corrals, one to a storage room, and one to Vasha's old room.

Gabrielle kept her back to that door. It was all too thin a barrier between her and the room's current occupant.

In the quiet, she glanced back at Grace only to find her frowning.

"What?"

"I've read about places that isolated their women, but I didn't think Osto would do that. It doesn't seem . . . equal."

"Oh! No!" Gabrielle's eyes widened. "It's not like—it's not isolation. It's for women—who, well, who don't want to live in their family allotments anymore. Like if they aren't getting along. Or for newcomers without families. Or, you know, if they just want a bed out of sight of their parents. There are single men's quarters, too. And anyone is free to move out whenever they want."

"Ah! That does make more sense." Grace took a moment to peek through the open door of one of the larger lots. It only had one inhabitant at the moment—the spaces closest to the halls tended to be unpopular—and the bare beds and empty storage crates looked particularly stark.

Gabrielle cast about for a response. "Devra lives over there. We could go see if she's in."

"All right," Grace agreed.

Two rooms down, Devra's space was cluttered with possessions and every evidence of lives in motion. Though no one was currently home, the four beds were covered in brightly striped blankets, and the shared table bore a small collection of motley earthenware vases, each holding a single bloom of a different type of flower. One of the roommates must have been a woodworker, now or at some point in the past, because the standard storage crates had been replaced with tall shelves beside each bed, all covered in carvings and whittling.

Grace took a quick look around the room and stepped out, giving an apologetic shrug for her curiosity. "It's very kind of you to host me while I'm here. I know Gemma has been enjoying her time with the Johnsons. You could have just put us in an empty room, after all."

Gabrielle laughed. "I'm sorry, I know it's a bit crowded. But I'm sure Amaya didn't want to risk you getting lost in the lots while you were here."

"Mmm." Grace's tone was oddly noncommittal. "Will you and Umair move to your own room when the baby is born?"

"The . . ." Gabrielle went pale as a hand rose almost automatically to her belly. "How did . . . ?"

Grace blinked at her. "Is it supposed to be a secret? You touch your belly whenever you're upset. You did it all through dinner."

Gabrielle could feel herself blushing a telltale bright red. "Is it really that obvious?"

"Yes." Grace quirked a half-smile at her.

Her ears went warm with the blush. "I . . . Please don't say anything. I haven't told Umair yet."

Grace's eyes widened. "Have you told anyone?"

"My mom." Gabrielle found herself staring at the ground. "I don't know how to tell anyone else. Not even my own family. Is that in your story?"

"In my . . . ? You mean Romeo and Juliet?" Grace gave a soft laugh. "I'm afraid not. The young lovers don't get that far."

"What do you mean? I guess you didn't get to the end before."

Grace shook her head. "That's what makes the story so memorable. They make plans to run off together, to escape the city, but there's a miscommunication, and they both end up committing suicide. It's a tragedy that ends up bringing the warring houses together."

Cold flooded Gabrielle. "What?! You told me it was romantic!"

"It is! Don't you think? They both die for love, and they end the feud."

"I don't want to be peaceful and dead!" Gabrielle shook her head. "How can people like that?"

"Didn't you and Umair run away?"

"We came back! We . . ." Gabrielle fell silent as she tried to figure out what she was trying to say.

In the sudden quiet, the sound of several heavily booted pairs of feet stomping down the corridor was impossible to miss.

Gabrielle's cold turned to sudden fear. She could feel her father's silent, unseen presence in the room beyond. For a moment, she was back in that fateful late summer night, trapped in a dark room, uncertain if Umair was alive or dead, waiting for her father to give her away to a stranger.

Grace must have misinterpreted her expression because she only tilted her head and asked, "Should we be getting back?"

"Wait," Gabrielle hissed. She grabbed the other woman's elbow and pulled her into Devra's lot. She placed a finger to her lips even as the light of a lantern shone through one of the thinner fabric walls. Grace gave her a quizzical look but stayed quiet, understanding that something was wrong, even if she wasn't sure what worried her friend.

Outside the lot, rough voices muttered amongst themselves. Gabrielle pulled Grace away from the open door even as she strained to make out the words.

"It's this one, I think."

"I don't see why we're even talking to him, he already failed once."

"We don't need him, we need his kids. And he'll help us, if he doesn't want to stay in that room for the rest of his life."

"They said the other village was small. I think we could do it without them."

"Well, I don't, and I rank."

"For the moment."

"I thought we didn't count rank anymore."

Gabrielle frowned to herself, concentrating fiercely on figuring out the conversation. By the shadows they cast, at least five men were clustered around her father's door. Large men wearing bits of armor—almost certainly newcomers. Most of the conversation had been between two of the unseen men, but the last speaker had been someone else—his voice was slightly higher and carried a petulant tone.

"We count rank when we're doing Men's business," said the first voice. "And this is Men's business, make no mistake."

"I thought the Men didn't exist anymore."

There was a pause before the first voice said, "Well, maybe we'll call ourselves something else once we have a new base. Old Ben isn't exactly who I want to be, anyway. Rotting away in here, not even the leader. He's gone soft and weak. Fuck that! Now shut it, let me do the talking."

There was the sound of a key in a lock and a door swinging open. Footsteps trooped inside a small, cramped room, and then the door was pulled closed behind them.

Silence.

Gabrielle caught Grace staring at her with wide, worried eyes. She was certain she looked much the same.

"What do we do?" Grace asked, her hushed voice still ringing loud in the sudden quiet.

"We tell Mom," Gabrielle answered. Then, a second later, ". . . and Headwoman Amaya."

"When?"

"Now! Out the back way."

"The back way?" Grace looked around the crowded lot with its single open entry.

"Come on," Gabrielle jerked her head at the opposite corner of the room, bent down, and lifted an edge of the fabric wall, revealing a second allotment on the other side. This one was a family home, tight with scavenged, patched, oft-repaired furniture. A garland of multi-colored rags crisscrossed overhead, suggesting a ceiling and giving the place a cozy feel.

"I thought we weren't supposed to do this," Grace whispered as she followed her into the room.

"We used to do it all the time," Gabrielle replied absently. She was frowning into the distance, trying to remember the Shelter's layout from this angle. "I mean, no, we're not supposed to. But you can't stop kids, can you? I think it's this way."

They picked their way through another four lots before a wall gave way to reveal a hall Gabrielle recognized. She breathed a sigh of relief that they hadn't taken a wrong turn or run into any of the sheets of corrugated metal that made up some of the oldest walls. Only one moment to catch their breath, though—then it was off down the hall, seeking one authority or another who could take this new problem off their hands.

———

Once Gabrielle and Grace had left, dinner finished fairly quickly. Cedric and the kids took the dishes back to the kitchens, granting Amaya a few moments of precious peace.

All too few. Gemma, the New Tacoman glassblower, knocked quietly at the doorframe.

Amaya drew a breath. She'd been dreading this. "I'm sorry. I hope you understand that I . . . I have to follow the prevailing sentiment. I represent the people; I don't fight them."

"It certainly isn't the outcome we were hoping for." Gemma somehow managed to look kind and forgiving even as she voiced her disappointment.

Amaya set her jaw. This, then, was the part of leading she would have to get used to. "I know. I'm sorry. It isn't what I would have chosen, were it only up to me. But we wanted to ensure all of Osto had a say, and this is what they said."

Gemma gave a faint smile. "I understand, Headwoman. Truly."

Amaya flinched at the title. She had never realized how precisely the mildest words could be used to wound.

Gemma, however, didn't seem to be finished. "But tell me, Headwoman Amaya. Do you honestly think there will be any seed left to send to us? I've visited your fields, and all I hear about is how worried the farmers are, how hard it's been since the raiders showed up."

"The *newcomers* have certainly been a strain," Amaya replied, putting a strong emphasis on the correct word. "But we are trying to handle it. And I think we can, so long as we don't encounter further issues."

"Issues like us," Gemma said. She had an uncomfortable ability to give voice to exactly what Amaya was trying to avoid. "Even though we came with offers of help and friendship, and a much smaller request than anything the *newcomers* brought."

Amaya just managed not to shift uncomfortably on the stool. "That's all true. Yet we can't exactly trade one for the other. The newcomers have brought skills and resources of their own that will make Osto stronger for years to come."

"But Osto isn't about being strong, is it?" Gemma's gaze was unflinching. "It's about ideals."

"Ideals still need to consider survival," Amaya replied. "What use is the most virtuous set of ideals if the people who hold them are dead? I'm sorry. But one of our ideals is democracy, and the people are speaking."

Gemma looked away at last. A muscle in her jaw twitched as though working to keep some reply locked inside. After a long moment, she finally said, "I understand, of course. New Tacoma will . . . happily accept whatever grain you might see fit to spare us."

"Later, after planting," Amaya almost hated herself as she said it. "We would be happy to trade for other goods. Meat, fish . . . crafts . . ."

"Of course." Gemma was the picture of magnanimity. "The Folk do not renege on our offers. We are happy to share our skills and knowledge with all. When some are bettered, all are bettered. Those are *our* ideals."

Amaya hated this. The necessity of turning away good people asking for help, the need to suppress her own preferences to represent those of the village—when she had accepted the nomination for Headwoman, she had never imagined it might force her to follow through on something she found so personally, morally wrong. She liked Gemma. She liked Grace, too, and Dan and everyone else she had met in New Tacoma. They all seemed like good, honest people. Maybe a little unwise in their priorities, or at least, a little out of step with the priorities of survival, but still the sorts of people the world needed more of.

She hated all of it.

"In the future," she tried, "we might consider closer ties. Perhaps we could build a road between the villages. Osto is always open to feeding and housing travelers."

"The future," Gemma replied, "is not what I am concerned with at the moment, Headwoman. My people need help in the present."

She stood. Despite her age, her back was straight and her posture steady. "I thank you for at least considering our petition, Headwoman

Amaya. Grace and I will return home tomorrow to share Osto's decision. I understand how hard it was for you."

"For me," Amaya repeated, unable to hide the bitterness in the thought. Then she scrambled to follow Gemma's lead, and she, too, stood. "Allow me to offer an escort, at least. No one should travel alone for such a distance. And I know many more of our people are eager to meet you all."

Gemma inclined her head slightly at that. "Of course. We'll hope to leave at dawn, Headwoman. Whoever wishes to accompany us should meet us in front of the Shelter doors, I suppose."

"Of course," Amaya echoed.

Gemma turned and walked off, leaving Amaya alone in her lot. She took a few steps aside and sank to a bed, finding herself suddenly tired. The discussion had been tense in a way she had never experienced before. Wrought, even. And despite Gemma's graceful acceptance, it still felt . . . open. Unfinished. Dissatisfying. Was this, then, what it meant to be a leader? No wonder Vasha had stepped aside voluntarily, and her father before her. How had they done this for years—decades, even? Anyone who *enjoyed* being in such a position for any length of time probably wasn't fit for it.

She had only a few moments to herself before a new set of footsteps approached. She kept her eyes closed longer than she should but finally took a breath and looked up, squaring her shoulders as the new arrival entered the lot.

To her relief, it was only Gabrielle Newsome—then, to her consternation, Grace of New Tacoma followed Gabrielle into the lot.

The need to play politics in her own home would be the death of her, but Gabrielle, at least, was a welcome sight. The girl—the woman, really —had a wide-eyed expression that Amaya recognized all too well. It sent a jolt of fear between her shoulder blades.

"'Lo, Gabrielle," she said. "What is it?"

"I—no," Gabrielle started. She cleared her throat, looking uncomfortable and . . . scared. It was a startling look on a woman who had been so clearly growing stronger, free of her father's influence.

Grace put a hand on Gabrielle's shoulder. "I can . . ."

"No." Gabrielle shook her head and drew a breath, seeming to stand up a little straighter. "Amaya, I was showing Grace the women's quarters when we . . . we saw something. Something we weren't supposed to see."

Her heart dropped. "Yes?"

Gabrielle and Grace exchanged glances before Gabrielle continued haltingly. "We saw . . . five, I think. Five of the newcomers go to visit my father. We heard—I think they're planning to try to take over New Tacoma! With my family's help, and I don't know how many of the raiders–"

The premonitory jolt of fear spread to a hot glow of fury.

"Allah yintaqim minhu," Amaya spit. She blinked, surprised at the phrase which had risen from the depths of her memory in the heat of her anger. "And I just told Gemma—no!"

"You told Gemma what?" Grace asked, alert.

"Nothing—nothing good." Amaya shook her head. There was no time for regrets now. No time to wish things had gone differently. Not if Gabrielle and Grace spoke the truth. "How many, you said? Five? And the Newsomes?"

Gabrielle nodded. "One thought they didn't need my family's help, but another did."

Her own fury surprised her. She had been willing to accept and carry out the will of the village, even when it went against her own preferences and beliefs—because that was Osto. Osto was about coming together and working as one. Osto was about surviving together, combining strengths, and welcoming all. Jon Newsome had shown time and again, now, that he did not accept this central tenet of the village they all shared. He explicitly worked against the people's will, to the detriment of them all, and she was no longer willing to put up with it. She was not going to let him shatter this first fragile alliance. She was the Headwoman, and she would lead.

"I need the two of you to listen to me very, very carefully, okay? Thanks to you two, we have the advantage, we can surprise them. Let's keep that for as long as we can."

———

Danica and Lani's small cottage behind the Shelter had never had so many guests, and all the grim faces looked especially out of place amidst the cheery homeyness of the honey pots and dried herbs. Yet it was the safest place Amaya could have asked for—one of the only places where they could be very sure they weren't being overheard by unseen listeners. Lani needed no urging to take Chloe out to the garden to play, but Danica sat herself down in one of the cottage's few chairs with an expression that said she wouldn't be moved for plague nor portent.

The others present did not yet know why they'd been summoned to the beekeepers' cottage, and they eyed each other warily as each new person arrived. It was a motley assortment—a representation of each of the many factions of Osto; people who knew *of* each other but did not necessarily *know* each other, and some even then unexpected.

Amaya was very much aware of herself as the center of this strange web of tenuous connections. Even if an individual strand wavered in support, she could only hope the center would hold.

That *she* would hold.

Sarah Newsome, quiet and kind, and, in some ways, the start of it all, sat beside her.

Vasha, stalwart and wise, beside her.

Old Ben, serene and somehow amused even now.

Drake, former leader of Esteben's Men, scowling like he already knew what would come.

Gemma and Grace, asked to act far beyond their expected roles, had the two seats of honor beside Danica.

Stan Johnson, to speak for the farmers.

Devra and Deetz, neither of whom had been explicitly invited but had somehow heard and filtered in. And beside them, George, for once without his shadow Ahmed.

The cottage was full to bursting. Amaya could only hope it would be enough. No time for speeches now—she would only have to hope that everyone present would accord her the courtesy of her station.

"Thank you all for coming so quickly," she started. She forced herself to continue without hesitation as she felt the room's attention focus on her. "And for your discretion. Time and secrecy may be the best tools we have to . . . to prevent a disaster."

"Well? What is it? Speak quickly, girl; some of us have less time than others." Old Ben could always be relied on to get to the point. Amaya almost smiled.

Almost.

"An hour ago, we discovered that some of the newcomers, the former raiders, are planning to invade our neighbors. They're hoping to recruit Jon Newsome and his family to the effort. I think . . . I think we can stop it, all of it, if we act quickly."

That prompted a burst of protest and reaction from the gathering.

Amaya watched closely, trying to gauge how each of them seemed to take the news. Drake, Deetz, and George, she noted, looked dismayed but not surprised. Devra, on the other hand, leaped forward, determined to be heard.

"Stop them, and then what? Imprison them along with Newsome? How long are we going to allow these dangerous assholes to live with us?"

By the time she finished the question, the others had quieted, and Devra took a deep breath, scowling as she schooled her words.

"Sarah, I'm sorry," Devra went on, "You're lovely, but that man you married is a traitor and a snake, and that's an insult to snakes. Leaving him was the smartest thing you've ever done. As long as he's around, he'll be a danger. And the others—the newcomers—" Here she paused and cast a look back over her shoulder at her partner. Deetz only looked back lovingly. "Well, some of them know what we stand for here in Osto. But others never bought in, not really, and we all know it. It's time we faced it and did something about it, and this might be our best chance."

A small chorus of support rose as she finished talking. Amaya raised her eyebrows at the lack of dissent. But then, she'd chosen her council with purpose.

"I think we are all of the same mind," she said. Then, "Drake? Do you have anything to add?"

Drake cleared his throat. The former leader of Esteben's Men was still handsome, though he was much changed from the arrogant raider who had arrived at Osto's door last summer. A hard winter of scant rations and long patrols had given him a rangy look, hollowed out his high cheekbones, and stolen the cruelty from his eyes. Now, he took his time to pick his words before he spoke.

"The Men joined Osto expecting an easier life than they had. For some, it's been everything we hoped for. But others only count food and riches, and they haven't been quiet about it."

"And what are we supposed to do with people like that?" Danica asked, frowning fiercely.

Drake shrugged. "Used to be they could challenge the leader, lose, and then get beaten half to death and left out for the wolves. But I understand you don't do things that way around here."

"Sure don't," Danica scoffed, but she didn't seem to have anything further to add.

Amaya cleared her throat carefully, taking the reins of the meeting back. "We do hold ourselves to a different standard here," she said. "But not necessarily a higher one. And even that, we have failed to meet."

There was a silence at this. Devra was the one brave enough to break it. "And what do you mean by that?"

She didn't like this. It felt like a betrayal, no matter what she did—either of her village, or of her friend.

But only one option had a better outcome for all. Amaya closed her eyes, sending a silent apology to Sarah, before she said, "The Newsomes were growing their own food. Hoarding it. And not just food, but resources as well. It was all discovered . . . in the wreckage of their house."

A murmur ran through the gathering. Danica and Stan looked shocked at the very idea. Old Ben, Vasha, and Drake did not. Beside her, Sarah Newsome sat gray and pale, silent, staring forward.

"Hoarding!? Even after last winter?" Devra demanded. She said nothing further, but the thought was plain enough on her face—*maybe some people do deserve the wolves.*

Amaya hurried to keep the focus of the meeting. "My point is that we are none of us blameless. Not Ostons nor newcomers. We together are bringing this threat to our new neighbors, and we together. . . what we do now, how we handle it, can determine what kind of community we will be moving forward. Do we tolerate repeated betrayals? Or do we draw a line on just how far we allow our values to be abused?"

"Jon . . ." Sarah faltered as those gathered turned to her. "Jon was always sure we had to look after ourselves first. He always thought . . ." She shook her head. "I'm sorry. We did not mean to withhold anything. He always said it was our own work and our own produce, so it wasn't like we were stealing."

The silence that greeted this was colder than any outburst could have been. Amaya moved an inch closer to her friend and put a hand on her shoulder, a show of support meant to both comfort and signal to the gathering.

"Sarah and her younger children have chosen Osto," she said. "They lived with us this past winter, and suffered and sacrificed with us, and for that, we welcome them. As we always have."

When no protest interrupted her, she pushed on. "It is time to make the rest choose. The Newsomes and the newcomers both. They need to either fully commit to Osto, or they need to leave and find their own place."

"Sounds like you're spoiling for a fight," Vasha said, her words dry as a bone, her gaze flat.

"Spoiling? No. Never." Amaya stared back at her predecessor. "But I'm not sure we can avoid this one."

"Osto doesn't fight," Stan said. "Isn't that the whole point of the Shelter?"

A chorus of muttered discontent rose, though whether it was for or against this statement was unclear.

"Osto *doesn't* fight," Amaya said, raising her voice to ensure she could regain the crowd's attention. "And Osto shouldn't have to. What we do, though, is defend. We protect. We nurture. And whatever else we might decide, I think we have an obligation to protect the Folk from our own problems."

There was a general mutter of agreement, punctuated by Vasha's, "Well, girl? Out with it."

She'd come this far. Amaya took a breath. "We have the advantages of time and surprise. And we also have some knowledge of the enemy, with Sarah and Drake here. So, here's what I propose. First, we need to erode Jon's support. Sarah, you talk to your family. The men, the women —anyone who might still listen. You tell them they have a choice, and they don't have to follow their father to their deaths. Osto takes care of its own. Even them."

Sarah Newsome paled, but nodded. "I . . . I think I know who to start with," she said.

Amaya nodded. She wanted to stew on that, but now was not the time. "Next, we need to show a unified front. Solidarity. Drake, we could use your help for this next part. I'm thinking of issuing a . . . a call to arms."

As he had done for a week now, Jacob requested a second serving of dinner from the kitchens. Today, it was a slab of millet bread slathered with a thin coating of rosemary honey. He had inhaled his own serving too quickly and found it hard to resist the second slice on its heavy clay plate.

But resist he must. Jacob walked with a slow, heavy tread across the open forum, skirting groups of farmers and trackers who had returned early from their long routes. He wavered as he approached the lots, then chose to walk around the outside edge—less likely to run into bright rooms full of happy families that way.

Just as he entered the narrow hall formed by the edge of the lots and the outer wall of the Shelter, a hand tapped on his shoulder, startling him so much he nearly dropped the plate. He spun around to confront—

His mother.

Sarah Newsome smiled, laying a hand on his forearm. "Bringing dinner to Pa again? You're a good boy. A good son."

"Ma . . ." Jacob heard the quaver in his voice and steeled himself. "We're not s'posed to talk to you anymore."

He made to pull away.

"You don't have to talk." Sarah released her hand, letting him go, and then nodded as he remained in place. "But it can't hurt to listen, can it?"

DAY 8

The delegation gathered in front of the Shelter was bright, upbeat, and *large.* More than forty people had answered the open call for an escort back to New Tacoma—forty people on forty horses filled the entire square in front of the Shelter, and their restive preparations for the coming journey filled the air with a frisson of excitement. It was still early, though the patrols had left for their routes already, and a nervous energy powered even those who normally greeted the morning reluctantly.

Grace watched with wide, worried eyes as Gabrielle tightened the girth on a black and white mare.

"Isn't that too tight?"

Gabrielle shook her head. "These things can never be too tight. Half the time, the horse is holding a belly full of air when you saddle her. It ends up being too loose, and you don't find out 'til you're upside-down."

"Oh . . ." Grace nodded, opened her mouth again, then closed it.

Gabrielle caught the motion and stepped in close to ask, "What is it?"

Grace shook her head. "Worry. Just worry, plain and simple. Do you think this is enough people? Or is it too many, and the . . . the raiders will get suspicious? Should we even be doing this, or should we try to pin them down here, where you have more people? And should you even be coming along?"

"What, in my delicate state?" Gabrielle snorted at that and waved off the concern. "It's early days on that, I promise. As for the rest of it . . ." She shook her head. "I can't rightly say. No one can, really. We've just got to hope we've got it right. Besides, they might chicken out and not do anything, right? Wouldn't that be best?"

"It would . . ." Grace shook her head. "But they'd still be here. They'd still be a problem."

"Along with my dad." Gabrielle scowled at the thought. "So overall, I guess it would be better if they do try and we can get it all over with at once."

"I guess." Grace couldn't seem to find much else to say.

"You're all good here." Gabrielle gave the horse a pat. "And I'll stick close in case you start to fall."

Grace managed a smile at that. "Thanks, I think."

————

Stan and Elise Johnson were arguing. They argued often, but mostly, they were light, meaningless disagreements: duties around the lot, or late shifts, or the relative merits of wheat versus barley. This one, though. This one had the makings of a historic blowout. A whispered historic blowout in front of the barn.

"You *can't* take him," Elise said firmly. "Not if there's any possibility of violence. You *know* how he gets around the newcomers."

"I can and I will," Stan said. "It will do him good. You heard the reports—they've got new dyes and fabrics there. He wants to see it."

"If it still exists in three days." Elise crossed her arms. "He needs to stay here where it's safe."

"It hasn't exactly been safe for him here, has it?" Stan crossed his arms right back, and they stood, eye to eye and toe to toe. He had married a woman who could hold her own against an army, and most of the time, he appreciated it.

"If the worst of the lot wants to leave Osto, I say let them," Elise declared. "But there's no call to go chasing them and no reason you have to go too."

"I do have to go," Stan shot back. "It's only right. The more of us there are, the safer it will be."

"Or you could stay here and defend your own home," Elise parried. "The more of us there are, the safer it will be."

Stan gave a growl of frustration at that. Both Johnsons turned, though, as their son approached them, carrying a small pack of clothes and supplies. Anton had improved since his injury, though not fully recovered. His clever hands were stiff and slow, his mind often even slower. The newcomers in Osto still terrified him, even months later. The sight of a black-clad man often sent Anton into retreat, his heart pounding, his brain telling him to run from the approaching predator. Even George, who always regarded him with nothing more than kindness, triggered his instinct to flee. Even Sirks . . .

Especially Sirks.

"I'm going," Anton said. "Please, Mom. It's . . . I want to go."

Elise quirked her mouth. It had always been hard to deny her only child anything, but since the injury, there had been so little he'd stirred himself to ask for.

"It's too dangerous," she managed. "You heard what Devra said. They're expecting . . ."

"They're expecting to hold off a small group of raiders," Stan finished. "A small group. Look at us! We'll more than outnumber them! And I'll be sure Anton stays safe in the back."

Elise caught her breath, trying to clamp down on unhelpful emotions. "That's . . ."

She took another look at her son. Her son, who had made this decision on his own, packed his own things, and now stood waiting to request his own horse.

She sighed. "Be sure you *both* stay safe in the back, you hear me?"

———

Amaya Bly and Sarah Newsome stood to the side of the wide, cleared plaza in front of the Shelter, watching the people of Osto gather. There were more than she'd expected, but not as many as she'd feared— apparently, the word had spread exactly as they'd hoped. No one was trying to bring small children along, but many packed bows, knives, and other weapons ostensibly for hunting. Families whispered hurried goodbyes to each other, lover to lover, or parent to child, or whatever other configuration they'd chosen. Many grinned ruefully at the thought of testing newly acquired riding skills on such a long journey. Jacob Newsome stood apart, holding the reins of his assigned mount, worry in his eyes. Across the square, Danica and Lani conferred with Vasha, who held Chloe. It would be the first time they'd been apart from her since she'd been born.

Amaya could only imagine what they were going through. She looked sideways at Sarah, only to see that the woman was already looking back at her.

"What are you thinking?" Sarah asked, her voice low.

"I know we all agreed," Amaya said. "But I still can't help but wonder if this was the right decision."

A few yards away, a ranger stowed a wrapped bundle under a saddle blanket. The result was lumpy and obvious, but at least not identifiable. Both women watched as he secured it.

"I think it is," Sarah finally said. "It's the choice that helps the most people and hurts the fewest. Isn't that what we strive for?"

"It is . . ." Amaya bit her lip. "I only hope . . . I don't know." She shook her head. "Too many things could go wrong. I hate this."

"Yes." Sarah turned to fully face Amaya. "But you didn't choose it. You're only coping with what was handed to you. And I think . . . I think it will send a good message. To the Folk, to the raiders, and to anyone who hears about it."

She couldn't help the small smile that prompted. "People do seem to hear about us, don't they?"

"And more will come," Sarah agreed. "And they'll keep coming for as long as Osto stands and as long as it stands for what's right."

Amaya swallowed against the lump in her throat. She was saved from having to respond when Devra and Drake rode their steeds out to the front of the gathered crowd, hastily appointed generals to their impromptu army.

"Who knew so many would want to join us?" Devra called, her voice pitched to carry over the masses.

Drake grinned, the expression holding only a ghost of the feral cruelty he'd once worn like a mantle. "It's a longer trip than most are ready for," he replied. "Are you all sure you want to come?"

There was a half-hearted, slightly confused round of assent from the crowd. Someone called, "It's too early in the morning for second thoughts!" The gathering chuckled grimly.

"Let's go meet our neighbors!" Devra called, and this got a much more enthusiastic response. "Let's give them a proper Osto welcome!"

Drake nodded at the growing cheers. "And we will show them what it means when Osto extends its hand in friendship and protection."

This time, the cheer had a low undertone to it, which Amaya hoped signaled determination. If nothing else, she was sure most people in the crowd had caught the nuance in Drake's words—the whispers had spread, and most, if not all, knew why they were really here.

"Mount up!" called Devra. "Say your goodbyes! We leave in five minutes!"

A final cheer broke up into a flurry of activity. Amaya sighed, her own gloom untouched by the speech. However, her grim mood lightened when she spotted Cedric approaching with Umair and Reggie.

"What, just three?" she asked, as Cedric ducked down to give her a quick kiss on the cheek.

"Jess thinks if she doesn't see you leave, it won't happen."

"Oh dear," Amaya sighed. She gave Umair and Reggie quick hugs— or meant to—but each held on longer than she'd expected.

"Bring us back something, Mom," Reggie said.

Amaya raised an eyebrow. "Something?"

"Something we don't have here."

She couldn't help but smile at that. "I'll see what I can do."

Umair's hug was longer and firmer. "Be careful," he said softly, and her heart melted.

"Look after your sisters while I'm gone," she replied.

He nodded solemnly, and Amaya had to look away before she spit out secrets that weren't hers to share. Cedric claimed the next hug, saving her from potential indiscretion.

"Sorry about Jess," he murmured.

Amaya laughed as they broke apart. "Someone's going to have to teach that girl about cause and effect."

Cedric smiled. "Maybe that will be our project while you're gone."

"You think you can teach her the entire history of Osto before I get back?"

"I think she'll surprise you," Cedric replied. He looked out at the crowd. "I think they all will."

Amaya just managed not to hunch her shoulders. She was quiet for a long moment before allowing herself to voice the thoughts that had been chasing around her head since the meeting in the cottage.

"Cedric . . . what if someone gets hurt? What if we've miscalculated, and it all turns awful? What if . . . what if someone dies, and it's my fault?"

In lieu of an answer, Cedric pulled her in for another hug. She let the firm pressure of his arms hold off the doubt for a few moments more.

"Some of that may happen," he said softly. "But if it does, it won't be your fault. Make sure . . . when you make camp tonight, make sure everyone knows what's happening. Give them a chance to turn back. Let them know there's no shame in it. Then you can be certain that whoever comes with you made their own choice, free and clear."

The words made sense. They did. Amaya tried to let herself be convinced by them.

"All right, mount up! We're off!" Devra's voice rang across the plaza, and the crowd bustled with renewed activity. Cedric broke the hug to give her a long, lingering kiss.

"My brave, brilliant wife," he whispered.

Amaya laughed. "My strong, responsible husband."

Behind her, she could practically feel Umair and Reggie rolling their eyes. In front of her, Sarah Newsome held her horse's reins and waited.

"All right," Amaya breathed. "Let's go."

———

The ride was no shorter the second time, and the darkness and chill, the tension in the air, and the urgency of their mission made it no easier. After the initial excitement of their departure, the group settled in for the journey in a strange sort of quiet. The thundering of hoofbeats and the jangle of tack made a background music that discouraged chatter, and even the rare few riders who shared a mount were quiet, letting the gloom of the day settle between them.

All but Lani and Danica. They both rode a large mare, with Danica forward on the saddle and holding the reins, Lani behind her, arms around her wife's waist for stability. Lani pressed herself to Danica's back, her eyes closed tightly for mile after mile. When the sun began its ascent, she peeked up, gasped softly at the speed and height at which she found herself moving, and re-tightened her grip.

Danica glanced over her shoulder only to see a mess of curly dark hair. "I didn't expect you to want to come," she said, pitching her voice to carry behind her.

"Why, because I'm such a homebody?" Lani answered. She sniffed. "You're not wrong."

Another moment passed before Danica tried again. "So, why?"

"I couldn't let you have all the fun," Lani replied. Then, "Besides, if we let George monopolize the glassblower, how will I get any jars out of her?"

Danica laughed, the movement of her diaphragm plain against Lani's arms. "Honey? Really?"

"Not just honey," Lani said, her pout somehow audible. "Baby food. Jams and jellies. Alcohol, if I can figure out the process. It could completely solve our food storage issues. Not to mention plates, drinking glasses, dry storage for herbs . . ."

"Okay, okay!" Danica grinned. "I'm sorry. I shouldn't have questioned you."

"That's right," Lani muttered. "Just steer the horse and look pretty."

"Try not to fall off," Danica shot back, the smile clear in her voice.

———

The group was large enough to break into three circles to make camp that night. As darkness fell, they spread over a wide stretch of the forest floor—something Amaya worried over but eventually decided couldn't be helped. Drake joined one circle, Devra the second, and Amaya the third. They lit no campfires but ate cold oats and bread for dinner. Lani shared a crock of honey around her circle, and it eventually made its way over to the other two. It returned to her nearly empty but put everyone in a considerably cheerier frame of mind.

Eventually, when dinner was nearly finished and people had settled into a low buzz of companionable conversation, Amaya cleared her throat.

"I want to thank you all for coming with us on this . . . diplomatic mission," she started. The small noises of the settling camp fell away; her people knew there was more to come. "And I want to make sure . . . that you all know why you're here."

Behind her, she heard Devra's voice rise above the others in her circle, and she knew that her two generals were starting the same speech in their respective circles.

"Yesterday, we discovered that . . . certain people in Osto—certain discontents—planned to invade our neighbors in New Tacoma."

A soft grumble answered her statement. There was no surprise, no outraged exclamation. The rumors had spread as quickly as she had intended. Amaya nodded, waiting for quiet again before continuing.

"It is my belief—as an Oston and your Headwoman—that we cannot be responsible for bringing danger to our neighbors. If we let them come to harm, knowing we could have prevented it, we are as much to blame as the dissidents themselves."

She paused, but there was no response this time. "Our goal tomorrow is to get there before they can. Thanks to Sarah and Jacob, we believe they intended to sneak off from patrol, and we made sure to give them the widest possible route in the wrong direction. We left early enough that we should have some distance on them, if we're lucky. The invaders are expecting to find an undefended village. We will change that calculation. I know many of you brought weapons. It is my hope that we will not need to use them."

"And what then?"

Amaya closed her eyes. The question came from Jacob Newsome. He sat next to his mother, looking pale and drawn. As he spoke, Sarah patted his arm in reassurance. His position was one Amaya did not envy, but she was grateful he had chosen it.

"Even if we run them off without a fight, what happens? Do they just get to go back home?"

Somehow, the answer was harder to voice when it was Jacob asking the question. "No," Amaya said firmly. "We have tolerated this dissent long enough already, and it has only led to the growth and hardening of their ambition. We need to face facts—if we don't defend our beliefs, we will lose our home as we know it. So, if these malcontents do try to go back to the Shelter . . . they will find it closed and barred against them."

This, at least, drew a round of soft, surprised gasps. "You're throwing them out?" someone asked in a hoarse whisper.

"If they don't want to live as we do, then we won't welcome them," Amaya said firmly. "If an individual wants to return, they can serve the same sentence that Drake did—the longest and hardest duties for a season, to prove that they care enough to stay. But they are the ones taking this action. They are the ones breaking with Osto's values, and they must and will face consequences for it."

"And if they won't leave?" That was Stan Johnson. Of course it was. "If they park themselves outside the Shelter and keep us locked inside? Or camp in the woods to steal our crops?"

"Then we deal with them as we would any other attack," Amaya said. She hoped the bravado in her voice rang less hollow to her listeners than it did to her. "They are the ones making themselves enemies of

Osto. We are only responding to the dangers they present. Proportionally."

"You told everyone to fortify the Shelter after we left?"

She nodded, though it was dark enough now that no one could see it. "Deetz and Sirks are in charge of defense for everyone back home. They agreed to wait until the dissidents left, then lock down. The dissidents have lost their rights to live in Osto."

Amaya paused a second, waiting to see if that drew any protest. When it did not, she drew a deep breath. "If there's anyone here who did not know what we were planning when you left this morning, I am deeply sorry. If you're not comfortable being a part of it, I understand. And if you wish to head back to Osto, George will be waiting to guide you back at dawn. You don't have to explain, and no one will think less of you. I can't ask anyone to . . . to fight against their will or for a cause they didn't know they were taking up. Though I hope there won't be any fighting, we still all need to be prepared for it."

That was it. Amaya waited, tense, for any further questions or protests, for argument or alternative suggestions. When none came, she heaved a quiet, thankful sigh.

"Thank you, all. This is . . . not something I hope we ever have to do again, but I am glad you are all here. Get as much sleep as you can—tomorrow will be a strange, hard day."

The night was long, cold, and sleepless for many. But in the morning, no rider joined George as he stood aside the encampment, and the full retinue swiftly packed, mounted, and set off for New Tacoma.

DAY 9

n the noonday sun, the Folklife Department's village looked much the same as she remembered it. Pennants snapped in the wind as motley wagons and carts settled into the soft mud of the riverbank. The skeleton of a new building had been erected since her last sight of the place—a low, round hut, it would be, soon covered in wood or the tough canvas of the wagons. As they drew closer, she realized something that made her heart ache—the Folk had spent the intervening days clearing fields they hoped to sow with crops, turning the dirt, and removing stones and debris.

Amaya halted her horse once she was well clear of the trees and turned in the saddle to watch as the rest of the Oston delegation emerged from the forest. She waved at Grace and Gemma when she spotted them.

"Come up front with me," she called. "We don't want to give the wrong impression."

Grace and Gemma rode older, placid mares that could be relied upon to behave with inexperienced riders. They ambled over when directed, far calmer than either of the Folk riding them.

"It just occurred to me that we may well look like an invading force ourselves," Amaya said. She tried to smile and failed. It wasn't really a joke. "Let's get you in sight so they can see nothing's wrong."

"Yet," Gemma finished.

Grace only nodded, her eyes wide and white.

As before, Dan Tallgrass came out to meet them. Unlike last time, he was flanked by a cadre of his folk in their bright garments, clutching hoes and axes—either tools or weapons, depending on the situation. They looked wary and confused but thankfully not aggressive.

Grace gave a soft shriek that might have been a name, slid off her horse, and darted to the side of a tall, sun-bronzed man with close-cropped hair. The two of them embraced without any acknowledgment whatsoever of the people watching them.

Something about the moment was so genuine, so heart-achingly familiar, that Amaya found an odd sort of reassurance in it.

Dan cocked his head to one side. "So? What am I to make of this cavalry, Amaya Bly of Osto?"

Amaya heaved a deep breath and then, taking a cue from Gemma, she too dismounted, hoping to meet the man on equal ground.

"I'm worried we've brought trouble to your doorstep, Dan. This—" she gestured behind her at the gathered Ostons— "is our attempt to fix it."

She watched as Dan considered her words and considered her.

He frowned. "Is there time to be more specific?"

"Hopefully."

He nodded and turned to the rest of the riders. "Then be welcome, all of you. Please, do whatever you think you need to do. Your Headwoman and I seem to have much to discuss."

The other Folk moved forward, laying down their weapons and offering to take reins or assist with dismounts. For a moment, Amaya watched the first true meeting of the two peoples, the first hesitant conversations between everyday Osto and their new neighbors. It should have been historic, something to savor and commit to memory and paper—but she had other responsibilities and not enough time. With a sigh, she turned and let Dan Tallgrass lead her into the nearest hut.

The structure contained a single room, like the other New Tacoman buildings she'd seen. It was crowded with shelves and crates, all meticulously labeled but shoved in at all angles any which way they might fit. Two of the heavy wooden crates had been pulled into the small central area and set a few feet apart—clearly, they weren't the first to use this place as an impromptu meeting space.

Dan waved her to one of the crates, and she passed by him toward it but waited to sit until he settled onto his. He took a moment to light a lantern hanging from one of the low beams.

"Well?" he asked. "At worst, I expected you to refuse my request when you returned, not to bring an army."

"It's not—" Amaya caught herself. "It's not what you think. I promise. Osto has nothing but goodwill toward you and yours. Although . . ."

He did not seem surprised. "Although we're not getting the grain we asked for."

She sighed. This part was inevitable. "I'm sorry. We simply can't spare it. This winter was hard on everyone, and our farmers are nervous enough about our own supply."

"Very well." The fact that he wasn't more upset only made her feel worse. "What else is there, then?"

"If anyone's in trouble, we can help," Amaya said quickly. "If . . . if someone's malnourished, or you need medicines you don't have, we'd be happy to give you whatever you need. And anyone who visits Osto will receive room and board."

"Of course," Dan echoed, his tone flat. "Why did you feel the need to bring fifty people to deliver bad news?"

Amaya bent her head. Her feelings were not what was important here. "I'm afraid . . . some of our people have decided the Oston way is not for them. A group, we think about thirty, but we're not certain. Some are former raiders. They've . . . decided they would rather return to raiding than live in peace. And they want to start with you."

Dan started to his feet. "I see. Well, they won't find us unprepared if that's what they thought. We can defend ourselves."

"We're hoping it won't come to that. Everyone we brought is prepared to fight, but if we're lucky, just the numbers will be enough." Amaya stared up at the ceiling of the building. Rough beams formed a twelve-pointed star, with the roof's peak at the middle. Beyond that, only canvas blocked her view of the sky. Outside, she knew more huts and wagons scattered across the floodplain. The whole village was wood and fabric and glass—far too easy to burn.

"That's . . . kind of you. All of you. Truly." Dan managed a faint smile, though it didn't reach his eyes. He turned, and his next words were muffled as he started searching through one of the stored crates. "But as I said, we can defend ourselves. We've been traveling since the last world ended; we crossed half a continent to get here, and we won't give up so easily."

Something in his words, his surety, sent a thrill of hope through Amaya. She found an answering smile and met his eyes. "If that's so, at least let us help."

Before he could respond, a cry arose outside—the raiders had been sighted.

———

When the dissidents finally emerged from the tree line, Amaya was surprised by how . . . paltry they seemed. After a day and a half of travel in a retinue of fifty humans and nearly as many horses, the twenty-some men that made up the rebel group were almost laughable.

And that wasn't even considering the Folk. Dan had pelted out of the hut as soon as the cry went up, bellowing orders and issuing commands. His people proved to be well-versed in the procedure—every time he turned, calling for someone specific, that person was already at his side, took their orders, and ran off to carry them out. If anything, it was the Ostons that disrupted the flow of events—Dan insisted they dismount, that the horses be led back toward the river, but the Ostons were loath to give up the advantages of size and speed that the horses gave them. It hardly seemed to make sense, given they knew the invaders would be mounted themselves, but to avoid an argument they could not afford when time was so tight, Amaya urged her people to do as he asked.

So it was that the dissidents were met with a long line of opponents on foot, a human wall between the village and the tree line, studded with weaponry both improvised and purposeful.

It didn't take long for both sides to recognize the wild disparity between them. The horses slowed, then stopped, still dozens of yards away.

From her position in the center of the line, flanked by Dan Tallgrass and Drake, Amaya squared her shoulders. This was no time to be fearful. And surely, surely, they could see how badly they were outnumbered.

She stepped forward.

Let them be the aggressors.

"My friends!" she called. "Were you too late to join us? We welcomed all who wanted to come greet our neighbors on this *diplomatic* mission."

There was a stir from the dissident group, and two rode out to match her. The one was so broad he seemed to overburden his horse. His bright hair, braided close to his skull in thin rows, shone copper in the sun. Beside him, Sorsch smiled with dazzlingly white teeth and bright gold hair, somehow out of place in the environment. Soon after, a third rider drew up behind them, and Amaya's back stiffened as she recognized Jon Newsome. When she looked more closely, she picked out three of his sons and in-laws and more of his older grandchildren amongst the riders.

Amaya heard a growl from behind her. "Redbane," said Drake. "And Sorsch. Why am I not surprised?"

Amaya gave a small nod but did not dare a glance behind her.

The one who had to be Redbane scowled. "Don't talk around it, woman. We can see we were outplayed."

Amaya thought about Vasha, old and disabled as she was, walking out alone to face a mounted army far greater than this one. The courage that had to have taken. The strength of mind. She raised her chin.

"I was going to offer you a choice," she said, her voice unwavering. "A chance to return to Osto and show your commitment through repentance. But Newsome, I'm afraid, has already lost that grace. So do any who conspire with him."

"Osto is weak," Redbane called. "And dying. Any who stay within its walls become mewling children, crying for a teat."

"A strange insult," Amaya said, almost to herself. "The thing about children is, they grow up. It is their main defining feature."

"Words," the blond one called. "We did not come here to argue words. But we also did not come to die in a futile fight."

"I will not return to the Shelter," Redbane spat. "No more thin stew, no more tasteless bread, no more fucking duty roster! The Men must ride again, but Old Ben is dead to us. We'll leave this place as Red's Bane!"

"Oh, very original," Drake commented behind her, and Amaya had to repress a smile.

"The Bane!" Sorsch called. He raised a crossbow to the sky, and an answering cheer rose behind him.

Amaya allowed herself to release a held breath. Would it truly be so simple? So bloodless?

No.

While the raiders cheered their new leader, one man's face grew dark and twisted with rage. Jonathan Newsome, the self-appointed third leader of the dissidents, sat on his horse facing the opposing line of his enemies—the wife who'd left him, the third child who'd betrayed him, and the brown-skinned woman who'd dared to keep him incarcerated. He sat and heard his allies agree to stand down, and he could not let that happen.

"What are you *doing?*" he cried. "They are right there! They are helpless! There may be more of them, but we have horses! You have guns! Show them!"

He made as though to lunge across the gap between him and Redbane, hands outstretched to grab the gun on the bigger man's hip, but he misjudged the distance, or else he was unaccustomed to sitting astride, and nearly overbalanced himself. As he worked to regain his seat, Redbane eyed him disdainfully.

"I will not risk my men in a fight we can plainly see we cannot win. Drop your warmongering. We are done here."

"We are *not,*" Jonathan snarled. He raised his own crossbow and called, "We will fight with or without you cowards! Newsomes, forward!"

The charge was a slow and confused one. Jonathan led, though with his poor riding skills, the need to stay seated won out over any desire to look intimidating. He managed to spur his mount to a gallop, but he clung to the beast's mane, a panicked look on his face as it sped forward. Behind him, his sons and grandsons were slow to start and slower still to encourage their mounts beyond a trot. None of them had the riding skills to hold or aim a weapon as they rode. The result was a staggered, almost aimless advance observed by two forces on either side that could not believe what they were witnessing.

"Well," said Dan Tallgrass, his voice flat. "Light it, I guess."

Amaya allowed herself to turn at that, throwing a questioning look over her shoulder, but the question was answered only seconds later as the fallow field before her erupted into roaring flame.

Every Oston present, whichever side they might be on, flinched back in surprise. The Folkies were better prepared, but even they seemed apprehensive, eyeing the eight-foot-tall flames and their proximity to the woods. The fire formed a wall between the New Tacomans and the advancing invaders—from her position on the ground, Amaya couldn't guess how thick it might be. Light and heat and searing sound—she'd had no idea how *loud* fire could be when there was so much of it—formed an impenetrable barrier around the village, mirroring the curve of the riverbank. The flames burned strangely white hot, and did not seem to spread from their defined borders, which she now saw as reburied trenches in the cleared fields. Amaya found herself thinking again of Gemma's glassware and Fantra's herbs. She wondered what other knowledge the Folk might be holding.

It was the horses that made the deciding call. Between their uncertain riders and the sudden appearance of flames taller than they were, the beasts panicked and bolted far faster than Newsomes could handle. The raiders were able to control their mounts to a degree, being further from the blaze and far more experienced riders, but the Newsomes were thrown to a man as their horses raced for the dark, cool safety of the forest. The thrown men sat in the dirt of the plain, looking dazed and, in some cases, pained.

"And that," Dan Tallgrass said, "is why we had you dismount."

Amaya could only nod in astonishment. After a moment, she found her voice.

"Leave, Jon Newsome," she called. "Not you nor any with you are welcome back in Osto now. If you go back there, you will find the way barred. You may take your horses if you can catch them, but you will not poison any more of our happiness."

From across the flames, Newsome spat on the ground. One of his large adult sons moved to help him up, and he shouted, only the vitriol carrying across the fire. The son backed off as Jon struggled to his feet.

One by one, the Newsome men picked themselves up. Dazed, slow, they conferred amongst themselves as their father railed, unintelligible. Then, as one, they raised their hands before them and turned to the wall of flames.

Jon Newsome snarled something, some final deprecation, and turned his back on the village, on his children, on his erstwhile neighbors, and limped off into the forest after the horses.

Amaya smiled and felt only the warmth of the fire.

The bonfire that night was the loudest, grandest, most triumphant affair anyone present could remember witnessing. The last of the trail rations from Osto combined with the fish and preserves of the Folk made for inventive, if not always successful, dishes, but no one seemed to mind when the music played loud and long, and the drink flowed freely.

It did not take long for the Folk and their Oston visitors to discover a wealth of shared songs across their various memories, though more often than not, attempts to sing them devolved into intense discussions of variations in chorus and lyrics.

Lani's honey made her instantly the most popular of the Ostons present. Folkies gathered around, eager to taste each concoction on offer and give her their own suggestions on uses and flavorings. Only the oldest of them could ever remember having tasted it before, and they swore that the memory paled compared to the real thing.

Danica stuck close to her wife's side, so close that Lani actually pushed her away with a playful shove.

"Relax, love, no one's going to whisk me away."

"I'm more worried about them whisking away everything you brought," Danica muttered.

Lani laughed. "I only brought what we could spare. The bees will make more, right? And it's important to start things off right. Sweet and clear."

"It's . . ." Danica blinked. "Is this still just about honey?"

"My dearest, darling wife." Lani leaned in close and kissed her cheek, which resulted in a cheer from her surrounding admirers. "It has never just been about honey, and you know that."

———

Amongst the celebrations, Anton found himself at loose ends. The joy of the riverside village bustled around him. The strangers all seemed to know exactly what they wanted to do and where they wanted to be. His father was caught up in intense conversations with new friends, and no one gave him more than a curious glance as they ate, talked, and sang.

He had never felt more out of place in his life. He'd never seen so many strangers before—before last winter, he'd never seen more than one or two new people at a time find their way to Osto, and the arrival of the raiders hadn't exactly been—he jerked his thoughts away from that subject before they found the dark, well-worn track he knew so well.

Busy people, large tents, sturdy wagons. New Tacoma was a village, for certain, but it was nothing like Osto. It was almost inside out—Osto kept its treasures hidden away inside the Shelter walls, safe and protected, but New Tacoma had spilled its gems onto the ground, bright and colorful for all to see. Every instinct Anton had screamed that this place could never continue, could never survive, could never hope to grow and thrive . . .

And yet, here it was.

A burst of husky voices broke into the heavy beats of a working song. Anton spotted the singers across the central plaza—a group of Folk, slightly older than he, sat with Jacob Newsome and a few of the newcomers he didn't know. As he watched, their song dissolved into a mumble of forgotten words and then laughter.

Yet the music continued. Anton frowned to himself, listening hard to pick out the melody that still hung in the air. It was an instrument, but not one he recognized. The music drew him across the plaza, past the singers. He supposed they, too, had picked up the melody.

A few moments later, he found himself before a tent. This one was on the smaller side, about the size of two family lots. Anton wondered if these people had allotments, or if they had found some other arrangement for living space.

The tent was a dull green that tended toward brown along the lines of folds and seams. It could have been made with any number of dyes; it was too faded now to tell the original hue. But someone had taken the time to embroider the edges with a dark red thread that he recognized as a beet-root dye. The embroidery looped and swirled in no particular pattern, creating a fluid design that seemed intentional nonetheless.

And the music continued from just the other side of the flaps hanging across the entrance. An instrument he'd never seen before gave the notes a distinctive thrum. Not a pipe or drum, or any of the whistles they had back home. This was more like the sound of a thin thread stretched taut and plucked. The song was fast and confident—clearly, the musician knew exactly what they were doing. As Anton listened, he recognized the beginning of the refrain he'd heard from the singers.

He wrung his hands, unconsciously running his left fingers across his right palm and feeling the ridge of new flesh there. When the song ended, he raised his fist to knock, realized there was no knocking on the heavy fabric of the tent, and instead called, uncertainly, "Hello?"

"'Lo?" came the response. "Come on in."

No turning back now. Anton bit his lip, forced himself to stop, and pushed the flap open.

Inside, it was so dim at first he couldn't see a thing. He blinked a few times, and his eyes slowly adjusted. Open slits in the roof of the tent let in enough light for him to see that the whole place was one open room. It was sturdier than he'd realized—the fabric walls were supported by a wooden frame of thick beams that looked strong and surprisingly permanent, and the floor was an elevated platform that he had to step up onto. A low bed, a number of shelves and chests, a rack of fishing equipment—

—and a girl, looking a few years older than he, with short-cropped dark hair and a wry expression in her large eyes. She sat on one of two chairs grouped around a small table, and she held what had to be the mystery instrument. It was an odd thing—a long neck protruded from a flat-fronted body, but a hole in the body was dark, suggesting it was not as flat as it looked from the front. Strings stretched across the entire thing, and as he watched, the girl pressed her hands flat against them, and the last notes hanging in the air abruptly ended.

"Oh," she said. "I didn't—I guess you're one of the visitors? From Osto?"

Anton nodded. His throat was suddenly dry. Why had he done this? What was he going to say?

"Nice to meet you!" The girl smiled widely. "I'm Sheena."

He swallowed, suddenly realizing this was the first girl remotely close to his age that he'd ever had to introduce himself to. "A . . . Anton."

"Welcome to New Tacoma, Anton!" She smiled.

He nodded but couldn't think of what to say.

Sheena's smile faltered a bit. "Can I . . . can I do anything for you? Are you lost?"

He shook his head quickly. Then, remembering what had drawn him to the tent in the first place, he nodded once.

She raised her eyebrows. "Well?"

Anton swallowed again, then, deciding he may as well get it over with, gestured at the instrument. "What *is* that?"

"Oh. Uh." She blinked. "It's called music."

He flushed. "I know that. I meant *that*." He pointed at the instrument again, then blushed deeper when he realized what he must sound like.

"Oh." She gave a sheepish laugh. "It's a guitar. An old one."

"Old? From before?" That explained its strange looks.

She nodded. "We have a few of them. We try to preserve them as best we can. Sit. Listen."

He sat.

She ran her fingers across the strings, and a liquid fall of notes followed. Anton's eyes widened. His fingers nearly itched to try it himself, but he was too well-trained a weaver to reach for strings he didn't understand.

"Wouldn't it be, uh, safer to keep it locked up somewhere? It would last longer if no one touched it."

Sheena laughed, and her laughter almost echoed the soft music she plucked out. "If an instrument is never played, can it truly be said to still be an instrument? If it sits locked in a box, what use is it? What's the difference between that and no guitar at all?"

"That's . . ." Anton frowned, thinking that over. It was a new idea, but he could feel the inherent rightness of it. After all, a loom that sat unwarped was worse than useless—it was a waste of precious space. "But what happens if it breaks?"

She shrugged and pressed her hand flat to the strings, stopping the soft notes once again. "Then we try to repair it. These strings break all the time, but we have a lot of replacements for them. Music is meant to be heard. Instruments are meant to be played. The old timers, they knew so many ways to make beauty."

Anton nodded. His eyes fixed on the strings, the box of the instrument, and what he now saw to be delicate carvings in the wood.

Sheena smiled. "Would you like to try it?"

He almost jerked backward at the question. "Me?"

"You." She grinned and held the guitar out to him. "I can see you have the itch. Go on. I trust you."

He hesitated, and she held her position, the instrument suspended between them like an offering. When it was plain she wasn't going to renege, Anton reached out and took it from her, carefully copying her hand position—one under the neck, one over the bulbous body.

"It's light!" he exclaimed. He had to quickly adjust his expectations; the guitar was almost buoyant when he'd been braced for weight. Carefully, he held the instrument close to him, cradling it the way the girl had.

Sheena smiled, but it didn't seem to have any mockery to it. "Keep your hand there, on the bottom, and play a chord. It's so thin you can feel the sound through the wood."

Anton didn't know what a chord was, but he took a guess and passed his fingers over the strings the way she had. A cacophony of notes resulted. The body of the instrument thrummed, just as she'd promised.

"Now, hold on." She leaned forward and, placing her hands over his, adjusted the positioning of the guitar. With the base of it perched in his lap, she maneuvered his free hand over the strings and more carefully set his left on the neck of the guitar. His palm burned under her touch, but for the first time in months, it had nothing to do with scar tissue.

"There," she said. "And if you press down there, you can change the tone."

He did as she suggested, and the notes sounded almost right this time. A grin, unbidden, sprang to his lips.

She grinned back. "There you go! That's the start of it. Now, have you ever learned to read music?"

"Read . . . music?" he repeated.

"Hold on, let me get something."

It sounded like a promise, and Anton let himself believe it might be fulfilled.

————

Late in the night, Amaya could not stop watching the younger set. A handful of Osto's older teens had come to defend their neighbors. Now, they met with the New Tacoman youth and quickly fell into the sorts of serious conversations and social games that only made sense to the young. Folkie children played near them, curious about the Ostons but kept at bay by their older compatriots.

The children. Amaya could not keep her eyes off the children. Toddlers roamed freely through the festivities, loosely supervised by those only a few years older. They hid behind their parents' legs, then burst forth, giggling madly and chasing each other across the square. Two small ones, almost certainly siblings, sat under a bench near the back of the crowd and babbled together over a stolen, near-empty tun of honey. A girl, maybe seven years old, had assigned herself the solemn duty of pouring drinks for anyone who approached the bench piled with cups and pitchers. She poured slowly, her hands shaking a little with the weight, and nodded proudly as she topped each glass.

How were there so many children in a village a quarter the size of

Osto when little Chloe had never even seen anyone her own age? Who would her future grandchild have to play with? If this alliance fell through . . .

How could she live with herself if she refused to feed so many children?

The village had spoken against it.

We all have a better chance at making it when we work together.

The village had also voted for *her*. What good was she, what was the point of her position, if she didn't trust her own judgment?

Amaya reached up to discover tears running down her face. Uncalled for. "Fine," she muttered to herself. "Fine. Fine!"

Dan Tallgrass sat on the other side of the bonfire, deep in conversation with one of his people. He looked up in surprise when she rapped on his shoulder.

"You'll get your grain," Amaya said, certainty in her tone. "If it's the last thing I do as Headwoman, you're getting your grain. I swear it."

END

EPILOGUE: DAY 183

"Here you go!" Umair held out slice of thick, brown bread.

Gabrielle took it from him, sighing in mock-frustration. "I'm not so useless yet that I can't wait in a line."

"Just because you can doesn't mean you should have to." Umair grinned. "Besides, this is temporary, right? Just think how busy we'll be once she arrives."

"She?"

Umair shrugged. "Or he. Or they. The point is, they'll keep us so busy you'll wish there was a line to wait in."

"Are you going to eat that, or just talk?" Devra and Deetz had followed close behind Umair, each carrying their own slices. Devra's kitten Yarrow clung to her shoulder, digging tiny claws into a pad added just for that purpose. The kitten had opinions—she kept stretching down Devra's shirt to sniff at the bread, seemingly deciding it was not worthy of her attention, and scrambling back up to her shoulder, only to repeat the whole process a few seconds later.

Gabrielle nodded over her shoulder. "I think Mom's setting up over there. She'll want us near her for the speech."

"Ugh, right." Devra grimaced, but with Deetz's hand at her waist, she followed Gabrielle and Umair across the green.

It was a brilliant autumn day, just settling into the long, cool end of summer. The sky was a clear blue unlike anything that could be seen out west, and the high sun promised more heat in the late afternoon, but also promised the safety of cool shaded woods and full creeks. On the broad green hillside above the river, the full complement of two villages gathered, feasted, and talked. The small group made their way to the front of the communal green, where several rows of benches had been installed much like the New Tacoma village center, though the crowd today far outnumbered the available seats. Her mother was already there, along with George, Drake, and Stan Johnson.

No sooner had Gabrielle taken her seat than she spotted young Ahmed. He ghosted along behind the back row of benches, exchanging only cursory greetings with those that called to him before moving on. He seemed to be trying to get a good look at everyone present, though occasionally he'd stop, frown, and note something down on a sheet of well-worn paper.

"What's he doing? He should be happier than anyone today, right?"

She asked the question of Umair, but it was George that answered. "Doesn't think the mill is calibrated right yet. Thinks the flour's too coarse. He's trying to figure out if everyone likes it."

That prompted Gabrielle to finally try her slice. Umair had slathered it with a jam she didn't recognize, but the tart berry flavor was a welcome contrast to the rich heaviness of the bread. She chewed with deep appreciation, imagining that, somehow, she could taste the captured warmth of the sun in the preserved fruit.

"The bread is perfect," she said. She opened her eyes only to see Ahmed staring at her intently, and she gave him a nod and a smile. "It's better than anything we've had in months. And how long did it take?"

George shrugged. "That first batch was a test run. Fifty loaves worth of flour in thirty minutes. Took longer to sift it." Though he was trying to sound nonchalant, his pride was evident.

"Fifty . . . !" Gabrielle shook her head. "Does he even realize how much this will change things?"

"He intends for it to change more than just breadmaking," George said.

He did not have a chance to explain any further, as Amaya Bly and Dan Tallgrass, flanked by Drake and Gemma, stepped onto the green, in full view of the gathered celebrants. Dan and Amaya each carried something that looked like a round metal shield three feet across, though Amaya's had clearly been hammered and shaped from a scavenged iron sheet. Dan's, on the other hand, was a bright bronze that shimmered in the sun. They grinned at each other, set their grips, and clapped the two halves of the cymbal together. The resulting clash seemed all the louder for the silence that followed, and the two leaders turned to face their people.

"My friends and neighbors," Amaya began. She glanced at Dan.

"Neighbors and friends!" He echoed.

"Welcome to the first day of operation of the New Alliance Mill!"

The last word was lost in the sound of three hundred people cheering simultaneously, feasting on bread and honey, and for once, allowing themselves to believe in the bright, full promise of the present day.

ACKNOWLEDGMENTS

Many thanks to my parents, Barry and Judy Newton, without whom I could never have gotten this far. Sic itur ad astra. Thank you also to Rachel Simko, my sister of the heart. And special thanks to Richard Fischer, whose invaluable advice on beekeeping enriched this work.

I would of course also like to thank Holly Lyn Walrath for her careful guidance and infinite patience, as well as the staff of Interstellar Flight Press for their tireless efforts: Elliot Brooks, Charlotte Cowie, Brianne Downing, Jamileh Jemison, Cassandra Rose Clarke, and J.B. Rockwell.

ABOUT THE AUTHOR

Meridel Newton has been a teacher, a researcher, a writer, and an editor. Now she lives in Washington, DC and dreams of cats and dragons. She is the author of the young adult novel The Puppet Kingdom, and her fiction has been included in anthologies such as 1001 Knights and Recognize Fascism. She is an alumna of the Futurescapes Writers' Workshop and a member of the Science Fiction & Fantasy Writers Association. When she is not reading or writing, she can be found online at thepuppetkingdom.com.

INTERSTELLAR FLIGHT PRESS

Interstellar Flight Press is an indie speculative publishing house. We feature innovative works from the best new writers in science fiction and fantasy. In the words of Ursula K. Le Guin, we need "writers who can see alternatives to how we live now, can see through our fear-stricken society and its obsessive technologies to other ways of being, and even imagine real grounds for hope."

Find us online at www.interstellarflightpress.com.

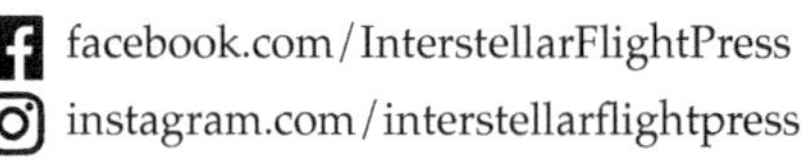

facebook.com/InterstellarFlightPress
instagram.com/interstellarflightpress